THE CRYPTIC LINES

Richard Storry

By the same author:
Order of Merit

The Cryptic Lines

First published 2015 by Cryptic Publications.
Second edition published 2015.
Cover design by Gergö Pocsai

ISBN: 150848841X
ISBN 13: 9781508488415

The Cryptic
Lines

PROLOGUE

I've paid for your sickest fancies;
I've humoured your crackdest whim-
Dick, it's your daddy, dying;
You've got to listen to him!
Good for a fortnight, am I?
The doctor told you? He lied.
I shall go under by morning, and -
Put that nurse outside.
Never seen death yet, Dickie?
Well, now is your time to learn,
And you'll wish you held my record
Before it comes to your turn.

- Rudyard Kipling

1

1960 – A remote coastal location, somewhere in the British Isles

T he night it all began there was nothing foreboding to see - at first.

But the damp, clinging atmosphere was thick and heavy.

Had you been standing there trying, in vain, to see through the impenetrable darkness with lashing rain repeatedly stinging your face, the cold combined chills of uncertainty, fear and danger were unmistakable. As your torch light flickered and died you would have wrapped your cloak tightly about you as the wind howled, and peered as deeply as you could into the surrounding gloom and murk hoping that, somehow, you might glimpse a way by which you could leave this place with its unbearable sense of dread.

And, as you resigned yourself to a seemingly interminable wait for the blessed return of the sun's illuminating rays, the thick darkness would have been dispelled suddenly as a tumultuous thunder clap tore the heavens apart and a simultaneous flash of lightning broke through, revealing, for just a fleeting moment, the grey forbidding edifice of Heston Grange.

Through the maelstrom you would have seen, but only for a second, the crumbling edges of what had once been proud and well defined masonry. Gargoyles, almost shapeless now, staring with sightless eyes guarding what had once been a magnificent dwelling. The large, unwelcoming arched oak door, with a rarely used rusty bell-pull to one side, standing defiantly closed.

And, currently at quite some distance behind the house, when the screeching wind momentarily ceased its violent assault, you would have heard the churning and swirling of the huge oceanic waves crashing and tearing into the base of the cliffs, slowly but surely eroding the rock away and bringing Heston Grange inch by resolute inch nearer to the edge.

Had you been there you would have seen all this.

But you were not there that night.

That privilege belonged, instead, to Charles Seymour, solicitor, who cursed as he fumbled with his keys in the rain and wind but eventually managed to lock the door of his Jaguar MK2; and, with upturned collar and his buffeted head bent into the howling storm, moved as quickly as he could across the unlit courtyard, but not without splashing through numerous muddy puddles on his route to the front door.

This sprawling gothic mansion was home to Lord Alfred Willoughby, a recluse of uncertain age. Although he must surely have been well into his eighties he was still physically agile, and in full possession of his mental faculties, though he allowed no visitors. Apart from himself, the only people present in the rambling old manor were his butler and housekeeper. Even the groundsman who, it must be said, did not do a particularly good job, did not live on site.

As His Lordship's solicitor, Charles had visited Heston Grange a number of times over the last few years, usually in response to a brusque summons by telephone which - he had come to recognise the tone of voice now - usually meant that either some person or organisation had committed what he perceived to be some heinous crime;

and the inevitable repercussion of this was a decision by the old gentleman to amend his last Will and Testament. Not that Charles was complaining, of course; the old boy never once questioned his fees, even though his services were priced at the more expensive end of the market. Privately, he was fairly certain that part of the reason Lord Willoughby kept him in employment was precisely because his fees were so high; and his reasoning on this matter was quite simple: why spend two days working for two clients when he could work one day for His Lordship and charge twice the fee?

Even so, financial advantages notwithstanding, he did not relish these visits which - and Lord Alfred was adamant about this - always had to take place at night. True, he was always received in suitably hospitable fashion, often with a good meal thrown in - but he was unable to shake the uncanny sensation that all was not well within these dank, decaying walls.

As he staggered forwards across the uneven cobbles the wind made one final attempt to get him to retrace his steps but, with what seemed like a Herculean effort, he managed to reach the door with a gasp and then leant back against it trying to catch his breath. For a moment he stood, staring out from beneath the moribund stonework of the porch into the violent storm, cold rain-water dripping from his every garment.

Reaching inside his sodden jacket he withdrew his comb and quickly ran it through his thinning hair - not that he was expecting it to do much to enhance his bedraggled appearance but it was better than nothing. He was aware that water had begun to seep into his shoes and a slight squelching sound could be heard if he placed too much weight on his right foot. Ah well, he thought to himself, let battle commence. He reached out for the bell-pull and gave it a firm tug. Deep within Heston Grange a bell swung on its spindle, which badly needed oiling, and a dull low-pitched clang announced his presence.

After what seemed an eternity standing in the howling wind Charles heard the faint sounds of movement from within and the sound of heavy bolts being slowly drawn back, along with the jangling of a large bunch of keys as several locks were released. At length, the door swung heavily and reluctantly inward and, although by now the interior of the house should have in no way startled him, Charles felt quite unnerved as he stepped gingerly over the gloomy threshold once again.

The entrance hall was dark; it always was. A large chandelier, which Charles had never seen in use, hung by three chains at points equidistant around its circumference, which disappeared up into the darkness to join the ceiling at some invisible point. The large hall-way was flanked by sweeping marble staircases on either side which curved up to the first floor level and joined in the middle to form a balcony. Numerous doors, all of which were closed, led to countless rooms with yet further rooms beyond those, none of which were used now. They simply remained, day after dismal day, echoes of what they had once been, filled with expensive furniture that must have been very fine years ago, but which was now gradually fading as was the very house itself, along with its occupant.

The door had been opened by James, who was the archetypal butler. Now in his seventies he continued to do his job well and was always very polite, and immaculately turned out. Charles had warmed to him the first time they met. More than once, though, he had wondered why someone like James would be content to come and work in a place like this for someone like-

Anyway, he had surmised, everyone has their own path to follow.

"Good evening, sir. Do come in. Looks like this storm will be with us all night."

"I think you may be right, James."

"His Lordship said to tell you that you'd be very welcome to stay the night if you didn't want to travel back in this weather, sir."

"Ah, that's a very kind offer."

"Oh sir, you're soaking! Please follow me; I'll take you to one of the guest rooms and you can have a change of clothes."

He picked up Charles' bag and moved towards the left staircase. Charles squelched after him with rather mixed feelings. Certainly, it was most kind of His Lordship to offer him a bed for the night, and he really didn't fancy the thought of having to venture back out into that holocaust. At the same time, however, neither did he greet the option of staying overnight at Heston Grange with much enthusiasm.

They made their way up the grand staircase and walked along the balcony, then up another flight of creaking wooden stairs to the second floor before turning left and right several times, through a veritable labyrinth of corridors until they were in a part of the house which Charles had not seen before. Lifeless ancient animal trophies stared vacantly from wooden shields, and antique suits of armour rattled slightly in response to their footfalls as they passed.

And everywhere there was dust. The place was thick with it. Charles felt that he didn't want to breathe too deeply in case he took in a lungful of the stuff.

"We're in the west wing now, sir; not used much these days. Still, it means there's plenty of room for you! Well, here we are."

He grinned as he pushed open the door then stood back to allow Charles to step inside. To his surprise, the room was quite welcoming. The room was of a modest size, but it was well lit, and a fire blazed in the hearth - and there was none of that wretched dust anywhere to be seen.

"You'll find the bathroom through the door in the corner, sir, and there's a selection of clothes in the wardrobe. I'm sure you'll find something to fit you." He grinned again.

"Thank you, James. This is all most welcome."

"A pleasure, sir. When you're ready, use the bell to call me and I'll bring you to Lord Willoughby."

With a slight bow, he left and closed the door behind him. Charles took a moment to take in his surroundings. The room was decorated with the kind of oak panelling he liked so much, and one of the walls was adorned with a large tapestry, very ornate and clearly handmade. It must have taken many months to complete, he thought. The carpet had a deep pile that shifted under his feet as he moved and the heavy velvet curtains across the bay window were of a comfortable deep theatrical red. But the centrepiece of the room was, without doubt, the elegant four-poster bed. The carvings which covered it were exquisite and the canopy was a mural depicting some ancient battle or other in fine detail. Well, he thought, I'm impressed. It was certainly a step up from what he was used to.

Being pleased to find that the unfamiliar shower controls could be operated without the user needing to possess a certificate from MENSA, Charles luxuriated in the jets of hot water, which were most refreshing, after which he found some much needed and suitably sized fresh clothing in the wardrobe, just as James had told him. He put on some grey slacks, a shirt and sleeveless sweater and a comfortable pair of black shoes; and then unceremoniously dumped the sodden garments in which he had arrived into the bathtub.

Before ringing for James to return, Charles thought it wise to have a final quick glance over His Lordship's Will, on the assumption that the whole point of the visit was for them to discuss some aspect of it. He pulled the twenty-page document from his bag, being relieved that he had seen fit to put it in a plastic wrapper before leaving the office; he was quite sure it would not have survived the downpour had he neglected to do so.

To put it mildly, Lord Alfred Willoughby was absolutely loaded. Of course, you wouldn't think so, to judge by the general state of repair of Heston Grange, but he had always been a shrewd old codger and, for safety's sake, was keen to portray an image that was not in keeping with his means. The fact of the matter was that this very private man owned one of the world's largest gold mines and held a significant share in a second. He also owned a string of oil refineries and had recently added another fortune to his pile through sharp operating on the stock market. All of this was in addition to the regular, and not insubstantial, income derived from property rentals on his two estates in Berkshire and Galloway. Not surprising, then, that as he was nearing the end of his life he was anxious to ensure that, after his departure, all these assets would be taken care of according to his wishes and in a responsible manner.

But the irony was that he had been nearing the end of his life for the last twenty years and showed no signs of checking out just yet. Consequently, his Will had been written and re-written, with each new set of amendments being based upon whichever of his acquaintances were in favour at any given time.

As he skimmed through the lengthy document Charles felt a pang of sympathy for his long-suffering secretary who, he knew, would be just thrilled at the prospect of having to type out the wretched thing yet again. Also, he wondered, who would be the lucky individuals this time who were about to get a boost to their future nest-eggs, and who would be the ones to lose out? Having slipped the pages back into the folder, Charles crossed the room and pushed the button to summon James. He heard nothing but knew that the butler would be on his way.

Having nothing to do now but wait for James to arrive, Charles idly stepped through the thick curtains into the bay window and stared out into the blackness. For the first time he realised that he was at the rear of the house since, away in the distance, he could see the moonlight reflecting off the restless sea, an inky black void that stretched far away in front of him. The rain was, if anything, heavier now and seeing such an untamed scene from the vantage point of a snug, warm room caused him to feel rather less tense than had been the case a short time ago.

His mind began to wander and he wondered, once again, about what he had done that caused his fiancé such offence that she had left him - was it really only four weeks ago? Whatever had provoked her to do such a thing? One bright, sunny morning, without giving any warning, she had suddenly announced she was leaving and, right then, simply walked out without so much as one word of explanation or even a backward glance. He told himself that there must have been another man, that it couldn't have been his fault; he had always looked after her and taken great care of her. He had.

Hadn't he?

As the now familiar morose feelings began to descend on him once again, he began to wonder for the tenth time in as many days whether he should perhaps be considering some sort of career change.

With a sigh, he was just about to turn away from the window when something caught his attention. Just over there...to the left...a torch light. Who would be out walking in the grounds on a night like this?... Gone again...no, there it is...

A knock at the door distracted him. He stepped back through the curtains.

"Come in."

"Feeling better now, sir?"

"Yes thank you, James. Er...James?"

"Yes sir?"

"I do believe I just spotted the light from someone's torch outside. Who on earth would be wandering about outside in this kind of weather?"

He gave a little laugh. "Oh, no one with any sense sir."

"Well, I'm pretty certain I wasn't imagining it."

A slight frown crossed James' face and he went to the window.

"Well, I can't see anything now, sir. It could have been a trick of the light, perhaps; happens all the time round these parts, what with the bad weather, the close proximity of the sea, and not to mention the moonlight and all."

"I suppose you must be right, but I'm sure I saw something."

"You know yourself, sir, how isolated we are out here. There's no-one else for miles around. Trick of the light, sir - that's what it'll have been. Shall I take you to His Lordship now? He's waiting for you."

"Oh, yes of course."

Charles picked up his briefcase and followed James from the room, not entirely convinced by his explanation. Still, he was here to see a client - nothing more. He'd deal with the business at hand, however eccentric it was, then leave as soon as was practical afterwards and that would be that.

2

James led Charles along endless corridors. Some of them were lit with electric light but some were illumined only by candle-light, while others were in virtual darkness. Almost all were of panelled oak, and numerous paintings hung in huge frames along their lengths. Lord Alfred loved paintings and was not a bad artist himself; but, with the notable exception of the obviously inhabited areas of the house, everywhere you looked was hallmarked by that covering of dust. As he followed the elderly butler, Charles was certain that the very lining of his lungs was being coated with it; and the place felt damp and smelt musty.

At length, he began to recognise some of the rooms and corridors again and, after ascending two more floors via a tight spiral staircase which opened onto another wide corridor, they finally stood outside His Lordship's bed chamber.

James lifted his hand to knock on the door but just as he did so it was opened from within to reveal Mrs Gillcarey, the housekeeper. She let out a small yelp of surprise when she saw Charles standing there, but curtsied politely and went her way, vanishing quickly into the dark catacomb of corridors. James explained that she would have been bringing His Lordship his usual nightcap, before he then stepped quietly into the room while Charles waited to be admitted. He could hear James and Lord Willoughby speaking in low tones, although from his position he could not tell what was being said. A few moments later the door swung fully open and James said "His Lordship will see you now, sir."

On entering the room, Charles needed to take a moment for his eyes to become accustomed to the light, or - more precisely - to the darkness, since there was no illumination at all in the bed chamber other than the light which emanated from a small coal fire in the grate. Through the gloom he could just make out the slight, still figure of Lord Willoughby lying outlined beneath a single blanket in his magnificent four-poster bed. James quietly tiptoed from the room and closed the door behind him with a soft click. Charles moved toward the bed, slowly.

"Your Lordship?"

No reply.

"Your Lordship?"

He spoke a little louder this time. There was a slight stirring from the frail figure, as the old man opened his eyes and turned his wizened, wrinkled face towards his visitor. He lifted a gnarled, damp hand and Charles took it.

"I'm glad you've come." His voice rasped in a guttural tone, little more than a whisper.

"It's always a pleasure to see you, Lord Willoughby."

With much wheezing and plenty of effort he managed to raise himself until he was sitting upright. Charles thought he seemed rather tired and quite unwell, noticing what appeared to be a coating of perspiration on the old gentleman's skin. In a careful and courteous manner he repositioned Lord Alfred's satin covered pillows to help make him more comfortable.

"Have you brought the Will?"

"I have."

"I need to change it."

Charles smiled as he pulled up a chair and sat down.

"That doesn't surprise you, does it?"

He shook his head.

"However," he continued, pausing for breath every few words, "I am optimistic...that this...this...will be the last time...I must ask this service...of you."

Suddenly, he was seized by a fit of hoarse coughing and his gaunt figure rocked back and forth uncontrollably. Taking a glass beaker from the bedside table Charles poured some water into it from a jug which stood alongside. Leaning over, he raised the glass to the old man's lips. Lord Willoughby managed to take a few sips and seemed to recover a little. He leaned himself carefully back against the headboard and took several deep breaths.

"Thank you," he said, simply, though with some difficulty.

Charles waited patiently while his client attempted to regain his composure. Lord Alfred was, without doubt, in a poor state of health - this was the first time that Charles had ever seen him like this. Normally, he was on fine form. After a few moments he spoke again although he was noticeably quieter now:

"Now then, where was I?"

"The Will, my Lord."

"Yes, yes. Of course."

Again, Charles waited a moment before speaking.

"How do you wish it to be altered?"

"That son of mine," he hissed, "My son. What did I do to deserve a boy like him? He never ceases to astound me with the deviousness of his schemes and with his dishonesty - the yardstick for every damned thing he sets out to ruin."

"My Lord?"

"He knows I'm wealthy, but..." and here Lord Alfred smiled wickedly, "he doesn't know *how* wealthy. I've managed to keep most of it secret." He leaned toward Charles with a sense of renewed intensity. "But I tell you this: I will not allow my fortune to be squandered by that no-good crook. He's a crook! That's what he is! Always has been! He's no son of mine!"

Again, Charles listened attentively as any good solicitor would, hoping that he would not take too long to come to the point. The fact was that Lord Alfred had never been able to have children of his own with his second wife and so, seeking to fulfil his paternal instinct, they had adopted two sons. The elder boy, William, had been a model son. If you could have ordered him from a catalogue, he was everything you would have chosen: intelligent, respectful, charming, witty and handsome. Two weeks after reaching his 17th birthday and buying his first motorcycle, he lost control on an icy road and collided with a tree. Lord Alfred had never really recovered from his tragic loss.

The second son, though, Matthew, was a different kettle of fish altogether. Whilst it all began with the best of intentions Lord Alfred and Matthew were like chalk and cheese. There was no love lost between them and as soon as he was old enough Matthew had spread his wings and fled the nest never to be seen again – except, of course, when he needed money. It was shortly after Matthew left home that Lord and Lady Willoughby had moved to Heston Grange. Even then, fate had another cruel card to play and Lady Willoughby, a frail creature who had already lost much of her zest for life following William's death, contracted pneumonia and passed away in her sleep during a particularly violent storm, not unlike the one which was raging outside at this very moment.

"But I've got a scheme of my own. Ha!" Lord Alfred continued his ranting. "My only regret is that I won't be there to see his face when he realises what sport I've made of him. Thieving bugger! Help me stand up."

"Are you sure you're feeling strong enough, my Lord?"

"Damn it, man! Don't you tell me when I can or can't stand in my own house! Here, take my arm."

Charles did as he was asked and supported the old man as he sidled to the edge of the bed, swung his legs over the side and slowly stood to his feet, albeit a little uncertainly.

"Give the Will to me."

Leaving him to stand alone momentarily, Charles picked up the folder from a nearby chaise longue and pulled out the document.

As he moved to pass it to him, Lord Alfred all but snatched it from his grasp, placed his hand flat upon the first page and formed a fist, ripping the paper from the binding. Without a word, but with determination etched on his countenance, he cast the crumpled page onto the glowing embers in the hearth where flames leapt instantly to engulf their new fuel. Charles stood and watched as he repeated this exercise until all the pages had suffered the same fate. For about the next thirty seconds or so, the room was lit brightly by the light of the flickering flames and, whilst the two men remained motionless, their shadows danced this way and that across the panelled walls.

As the flames gradually dwindled Charles noticed an exultant, almost fanatical, smile come to Alfred's face. With a grunt of satisfaction he turned and moved carefully back towards the bed.

"And now," he said, "I must tell you about my new Will."

Charles could not deny that following this passionate performance his professional curiosity had been most definitely aroused. His Lordship had always been a fairly enigmatic figure and watching him incinerate his Will in front of his eyes, when a simple written statement revoking it would have been sufficient, was high drama indeed. He picked up the folder and took out his legal pad but, as he did so, Lord Willoughby gave a sudden gasp and staggered uncertainly. Dropping the pad, Charles rushed to his side and took his arm.

"Are you quite well, Lord Alfred?"

"Yes...yes...let me be."

His breathing was laboured but he seemed to be recovering.

Releasing the grip on his arm, Charles moved back across the room to pick up the pad again. Without warning, Lord Alfred suddenly gave a cry of searing pain and fell heavily to his knees. The legal pad again fell to the floor, forgotten, as Charles raced over to his client a second time. He was clearly in distress. His face had turned deathly pale and his eyes were screwed shut in an expression of sheer agony.

"Lord Alfred, what's wrong? What should I do?" Charles screamed. "What do you need? Medicine? Tablets? Tell me!"

Lord Alfred was struggling to form words. He began to speak in a thin harsh tone, scarcely audible.

"...too...late...no time...please...the cryptic...lines...cryptic..."

"Your Lordship? Your Lordship? No!"

As thunder rolled and lightning flashed outside, a final strangulated breath was hoarsely exhaled and Lord Alfred's ancient body slumped against Charles. He lowered him gently to the floor before racing across the room to the servant bell, where he pushed the button frantically several times. With no way of knowing whether or not his distress call had been received he started to panic. Rushing to the large wooden door he grabbed the handle, flung it open and raced out into the dimly lit corridor beyond.

"James! James!" he yelled, "JAMES!"

3

In the daylight, Heston Grange appeared far less threatening - in fact, some of its rustic features gave it a certain character which was almost inviting. In the early light of the fresh morning with a gentle breeze coming in from the sea Charles walked around the entire perimeter of the house. Notwithstanding the fact that he had lost all sense of direction the night that Lord Willoughby had died, running frantically up and down numerous passageways screaming for help, from the outside the sprawling mansion was even larger than he had realised. Although he had been here many times over the years it only now occurred to him that this was the first time he had seen it during the daytime.

So, now that he had the benefit of being able to actually see the place properly, and having been left to himself to wander around for a while, the thing that arrested his attention most immediately was the extraordinary shape of the house; it was utterly irregular. The main central body of the building was, it appeared, of a slightly rhomboid structure having four storeys, inclusive of rooms under the eaves, and four turrets of different sizes spaced at apparently random intervals. The west wing, which housed Charles' bedroom, was more like a dog's tail incorporating several twists and turns before eventually opening out onto a yard bordered by a variety of outbuildings. At the east end of the house, but separate from it, stood a tower some fifty feet high and topped with battlements and a flagpole. Strangely, there was no apparent access to it other than by a rickety-looking wooden walkway that linked it to the main building at second floor level. Gazing up at it, Charles doubted whether it would take his weight; it looked almost rotten. Still, he made a mental note to ask James whether he might have a look inside this mysterious tower once all matters of business had been settled.

Lord Alfred had been taken away the same night. Rather than wait for an ambulance, James had driven him the 40 miles to the nearest hospital but he was pronounced dead on arrival. Both he and Mrs Gillcarey were obviously shocked, although they surely must have known that the old boy didn't have much longer for this world. However, since it was a sudden death, there would need to be a post mortem, meaning it would be a while until the funeral could be arranged. In the meantime, as His Lordship's solicitor, it fell to Charles to attend to matters concerning his estate; and so it was that he had come to Heston Grange for one night but would, in fact, have to remain for quite some time.

Whilst the number of administrative duties to be attended to were legion, his principal area of concern lay with the fact that His Lordship had, in his presence, rendered himself intestate. It was clear that he was just about to inform him of his new wishes but then-

Well, death has a way of thwarting the best laid plans.

Having waited for what he felt was a respectful period of time after his client's death he set to work sorting through all His Lordship's papers and effects. What a hoarder he had been! He appeared to have kept every utility bill, every invoice, every shopping list and carrier bag, every paper clip and every piece of string, bubble wrap and wrapping paper, and the operating instructions to just about every appliance he had ever owned since his first electricity generator had been installed. Every nook and cranny, every cupboard, every draw and receptacle seemed to house limitless quantities of the stuff. Most of it was pointless rubbish, yet it all had to be sorted through meticulously, just in case - by Charles.

It was as he was on his hands and knees, groping around inside the bottom of a large Welsh dresser and trying to extract yet another stack of probably worthless correspondence, that he discovered an old black box made from papier maché. Despite its age, it had the appearance of not having been used very often, yet it had obviously been opened recently as there were clear finger marks in its coating of dust. Sitting himself cross-legged on the floor Charles eased the catch aside and slowly opened the lid. The box was lined with a thin black fabric and contained just one item: a large brass key. Lifting it out, he turned it over and over in his hand, wondering.

Later, when James brought him his dinner in the dining room, Charles produced the key and asked him whether he knew which lock it was intended for.

"Oh, sir," he exclaimed, "Lord Alfred was desperately searching for this key just a few days ago. Wherever did you find it?"

Charles described the place to him although, for some reason that he could not quite pinpoint, he deliberately omitted to tell him about the finger marks on the box.

"It's the key to His Lordship's secret chamber," he said, "not that it was really a secret - that was just his name for it. Really, it was more just a place for him to keep his private papers really private. No one else was ever allowed to go inside."

"How could it be," Charles asked him, "that he could lose a key that was so important to him when he was the only person ever to use it?"

"I really have no idea, sir, but he was enraged when he found it was missing. He had me turning the house upside down searching for it, but without success. Luckily for Mrs Gillcarey it was her day off or she'd have been drafted in as well."

"Didn't he have a spare?"

"Not that I knew of, sir."

Charles insisted that James take him at once to this secret chamber and he followed him out of the room with the key clutched firmly in his hand, leaving his meal untouched – which was a pity, since it was a beautifully glazed gammon steak with perfectly sliced julienne vegetables, a delicious honey and mustard sauce and a crystal carafe of chilled moscato d'asti.

Back in the maze of twisting corridors, Charles followed James' lead and eventually found himself at a point where the wall was lined with many paintings. Lord Alfred had been an avid art collector, as well as being a keen amateur artist himself, and Heston Grange contained many fine pieces within its labyrinthine structure. James paused by a portrait depicting a finely dressed 19th century nobleman standing outside a shop in a busy street and, directing Charles' attention towards it, asked if he noticed anything unusual about it. At first glance there appeared to be nothing out of the ordinary - that is, nothing until he examined the shop door in the painting and realised, to his astonishment, that the keyhole in the door was actually a real keyhole! This felt like something straight out of a Boy's Own adventure story and, even though all he was doing was simply unlocking a door, the fact that it was disguised like this couldn't stop Charles from feeling just a little excited as he inserted the key and turned it. The painting or, rather, the door swung inwards on squeaky hinges and Charles found himself looking out onto the rickety bridge he had seen earlier which led to the mysterious octagonal tower. He was about to step onto it, but then he hesitated.

"Is it safe?" he asked, eyeing its apparently flimsy state of disrepair.

"Oh yes, sir, quite safe. It will certainly take your weight, if that's not too impertinent of me, sir."

The sun had almost set, its fading light glinting off the bobbing surface of the ocean, and the red sky on the horizon casting a beautiful hue over the landscape. With the evening beginning to draw in, just for a moment Charles wondered whether he should leave the exploration of this extraordinary room until the morning, but, as he looked at the closed door at the other end of the bridge, his curiosity now got the better of him. Somewhat gingerly, he placed a foot on the bridge and, grasping the rope handrails firmly, slowly began to make the crossing. The bridge creaked and swayed a little but, as James had predicted, it did take his weight and a few moments later he had reached the far side. While James was still following across the bridge, Charles tried the door. It was locked.

"I believe," said James as he approached, that you will find the same key will open this door too."

He was correct. The key turned and the door opened to reveal a darkened room with no natural light. They entered, slowly and carefully, just being able to make out the shapes of various objects semi-hidden by the gloom. James lit an oil lamp which stood on a reading desk in the centre and its glow revealed that the octagonal room was almost completely lined with filing cabinets. Against the one area of free wall space stood a drinks cabinet which was surmounted by a number of framed photographs.

"Lord Alfred handled all his business correspondence from here," explained James.

"It would have been useful," Charles replied, controlling himself with an effort, "to have known about this just a little earlier, rather than spending all my time sorting through old utility bills."

James looked a little sheepish.

"I am sorry, sir. Once you got started on all your sorting I thought it best to leave you to it; I assumed you knew what needed to be done - what with you being a solicitor and all - so I just kept out of the way. In any case, sir, you couldn't have gained access to this room without the key."

"Well, I think that the contents of these filing cabinets are more likely to furnish me with what I need to know than most of the other documents I've seen so far. I expect that I shall be working in here for quite a while and I may as well get started right away. Would you be so kind as to bring me some tea?"

While he waited for James to return Charles familiarised himself with the room. Taking a closer look at the display of photographs he was surprised to see that Lord Alfred appeared to have been good friends with a number of notable celebrities of years gone by. There he was smiling with Ava Gardner; over here was one taken with James Stewart. He could hardly believe his eyes - Lord Alfred attending the Oscars and being photographed with Clark Gable and Judy Garland. Well, the old boy had been quite a raver after all, thought Charles.

After this brief voyage of discovery he braced himself for a late night and, by the time James returned with a pot of rich assam tea and some homemade crumbly butter shortbread, he had already opened every drawer of each filing cabinet and gained a quick overview of the likely contents. Certainly, this was what he had been searching for, but it was plain that he was in for a long haul.

Finally, he turned his attention to the desk in the centre of the room. This had only one drawer, a shallow one which ran the full length of the desk just below the writing surface. Charles sat himself in the soft leather swivel chair in front of the desk and pulled the drawer open. Inside was a large padded envelope. He lifted it out and read the spidery handwriting on the front: *The Last Will and Testament of Lord Alfred Willoughby. To be opened in the event of my death.*

So the old boy had already made another Will!

On reflection, this did not really surprise Charles, although he did momentarily find himself feeling a little piqued that this new Will had been made without his being consulted. Nevertheless, the fact that there was indeed a Will in existence was certainly going to save Charles a lot of time and effort. But, as he carefully opened the envelope he was rather taken aback at what he found inside: A silver metal canister, with something rattling around inside. With a puzzled frown, Charles unscrewed the lid to discover a roll of Super 8 cine-film. Nothing else; no documents or papers of any kind.

Well, if the now departed Lord Alfred had decided to commit his last wishes to celluloid that was his privilege, but it was certainly a departure from what Charles was used to. This whole business is becoming more and more bizarre, he thought to himself.

The duty of the solicitor, as executor to the deceased, is to read the Will, ascertain who the beneficiaries are and invite them to attend a formal reading. On this occasion, however, Charles was not going to read it; he was going to watch it. Despite his curiosity as to what the mysterious film contained, he decided it would probably be best to wait until the morning so he could be refreshed when he viewed it.

Charles managed a good night's sleep, though he did find himself eating breakfast quite hastily the next morning - and then having to apologise to Mrs Gillcarey for not fully savouring the subtle flavours in her delicious eggs benedict. Risking an attack of indigestion, he walked rather too briskly to the library, although he need not have hurried. When he arrived, James was still setting up the rather antiquated film projector and screen. With nothing to do but wait he glanced, idly, along the long rows of books, many of which were leather-bound volumes and clearly expensive. Some of them were first editions.

His Lordship appeared to have been a very well read gentleman. The shelves ran the full length of the room, went all the way up to the high ceiling and were completely filled with books on every subject imaginable; and, unlike some private libraries, most of the books here had the appearance of actually having been read.

The poetry section - one of Lord Alfred's favourites - was, Charles noticed, particularly well stocked. All the greats of the poetic world were here: Auden, Betjeman, Blake, Browning, Dickinson, Donne, Frost, Keats, Kipling, Owen, Rosetti, Tennyson, Yeats - the list went on and on. The one wall which was not adorned with books was filled with small paintings: Portraits of literary masters, as well as various monarchs and explorers, each in an oval frame. These were clearly not the work of an amateur artist; although Charles was aware that Lord Alfred liked to do some painting of his own, he guessed that such offerings would probably have been kept out of sight, rather than risking being inevitably compared with such fine pieces as were displayed here.

Just then, James indicated that all was ready so Charles settled himself in a large comfy armchair, positioned his legal pad on his knee and sat with pen poised. After drawing the curtains, James set the film in motion then stood quietly and respectfully in the shadows. Sitting there in the darkened library, with the flickering light from the screen dancing in front of him, Charles began to view what turned out to be the most extraordinary piece of film he had ever seen.

4

After the projector had whirred to a stop and the screen had gone dark Charles sat in silence for a long time. Staring vacantly ahead, he seemed unaware of the sunlight that flooded back into the room as James opened the curtains once more.

"Sir?"

No response.

"Sir? Is everything alright?"

Charles seemed to awaken from his semi-trance. "Oh, yes. Thank you James. Everything's fine, thank you."

Just then, he heard something.

"What's that noise?"

"Sir?"

"Do you hear it? Over there...it sounds like it's coming from behind that wall...a sort of scrabbling sound."

All was silent again. They listened for a moment longer.

"I suppose it might have been Mrs Gillcarey, sir. She's always busying herself with some task or other; or maybe - oh, I do hope it wasn't a rat. We have occasionally had trouble with rats in the past."

"We may need to contact the pest control people."

"Maybe, sir."

After a few moments, Charles became aware that James was hovering with the demeanour of someone who had something to say but wasn't quite sure how to say it. Charles cleared his throat.

"Well," he began, "it would seem that my first task is to contact Matthew." After Lord Alfred's tirade against his son on the night of his death Charles felt a little surprised that he would be mentioned at all in the terms of the new Will; but mentioned he was, so that was that.

"Sir...if I may...?"

"Yes, James?" The elderly gentleman fidgeted uncomfortably as he tried to find the right words.

"Well, sir, it's not really my place to say, but...well...master Matthew, his Lordship's son, has always been...how can I put it? He has always been...well...something of a scoundrel, sir."

"That's as may be, James, but my duty is to carry out his Lordship's wishes; not to pass judgement on the character of those he names as beneficiaries."

"Oh, quite so, sir, yes. It's just that..." he faltered again.

Still seated in the armchair, Charles looked up at the loyal butler, feeling some sympathy for the man who had served his master faithfully for all these years.

"James," he said, gently, "if you have something important to tell me I can assure you that it will be treated with the utmost confidentiality."

James took a deep breath and then, with an effort, he said, "Well, sir, it's simply this: Whilst I have no intention of wishing to suggest anything...illegal..." he hesitated again.

"Take your time, James, I'm listening."

Now James seemed to summon his fortitude. He drew himself up to his full height and spoke.

"Sir, I do not wish to speak ill of His Lordship's son, but out of courtesy to Lord Alfred I feel I must inform you that master Matthew has been such a disrespectful boy. The only times he would ever make contact with his father was when he needed money - and it was usually a lot. Since, at this moment, master Matthew does not yet know of His Lordship's sad demise, might I suggest, sir, in the light of what we have just seen, that he need not know? At least, not until it is...ahem... too late? I am sure that between us we could work things out to reach a satisfactory arrangement for all concerned?"

"James, are you suggesting that I go against the express wishes of my client?"

"Oh, no, sir. Well...not exactly. It just seems to me that it would be somehow wrong if such a vast fortune were to find its way into the wrong hands."

"But James, they will be the right hands if that is what Lord Alfred has specified." There was a pause and James nodded. After this rare display of personal feelings Charles realised that James had now re-assumed his dutiful demeanour. Privately, he suspected that the but-ler's words were borne out of some bitter experience, but Charles was His Lordship's solicitor and he had a certain level of professional conduct to maintain. James raised his chin and spoke, calmly and politely.

"Very good, sir. Shall I locate a telephone number for master Matthew?"

So, master Matthew was called and informed of his father's death. During the telephone conversation, Charles noticed that he did not seem to express any sorrow or sadness at all but was, instead, ask-ing eager questions relating to the size of his inheritance. Charles was careful not to go into detail, saying instead that it was neces-sary for Matthew to come to Heston Grange in order to complete a number of formalities. He also mentioned that it would be advisable for him to come prepared for a stay of a few days due to the 'com-plexities' of some aspects of His Lordship's estate. There followed an awkward moment when Matthew said that, since he was the only surviving member of Lord Alfred's family, there ought not be any complexities; surely it would be a simple matter to arrange for the es-tate to be transferred into his name. His solicitor's experience came to the rescue and Charles was able to cloud the issue with some legal-sounding jargon. Matthew grunted and said he would arrive the next morning. The conversation was civil, but curt. Charles sighed as he replaced the receiver. Well, Mr Seymour, he thought to himself, just be professional. Do your job, and be professional.

It was at about 10am the following morning, and Charles was sorting through yet another pile of papers in the octagonal tower room, when he heard the sound of a car approaching outside. He stepped out of the room onto the rickety bridge just as the car - a silver Shelby Cobra GT - pulled into the courtyard. The occupant emerged. He was quite tall and in his mid-twenties, and he was wearing a suit that almost fitted quite well. Probably trying to impress me, thought Charles, although there isn't really any need. Matthew didn't look up and see Charles watching him from the bridge; he just made straight for the front door and gave the bell-pull a firm tug. Somewhere deep within the bowels of Heston Grange the reluctant bell announced his presence and the door was subsequently answered by James. As soon as Matthew had disappeared inside Charles went back into the tower room and quickly tidied away the variety of documents he'd been examining, before making his way back across the bridge, into the main house and down to the drawing room. As instructed, James had invited Matthew to take a seat and had offered him a choice from Lord Alfred's impressive collection of sherries.

When Charles entered, Matthew was reclining in a deep, luxurious sofa, holding aloft a glass of fine Amontillado, watching as the sunlight glinted through the amber liquid and the lead crystal vessel containing it. Ignoring what appeared to be certain airs and graces of this new 'lord of the manor' Charles crossed the room smiling, with his hand extended.

"Mr Willoughby? We spoke on the phone. I'm Charles Seymour, the solicitor acting for your late father. Thank you for coming. May I once again express my condolences on your sad loss."

Matthew shrugged. Without moving from his reclined position he reached up and shook hands.

"Although we do have quite a lot to attend to," said Charles, "there is no immediate urgency, as such. So if you would like some time to be alone, perhaps just to walk around the house and grounds, then please feel free - or I'm sure Mrs Gillcarey could rustle up a nice snack for you if you're feeling at all hungry?"

Matthew looked up and spoke for the first time. His gaze was firm. He didn't look like someone who had just lost his father.

"Thanks, Mr Seymour, but I'm happy to get started right away."

Charles nodded.

"Very well. In that case, would you come this way?"

He lead Matthew the appreciable distance from the drawing room to the library where the projector and screen were set up and ready in front of the burgundy-coloured twenty-volume Encyclopaedia Britannica, this time with two chairs positioned in front. James had already drawn the curtains so the room was lit with electric lights. Matthew seemed puzzled, then he sniggered.

"What's all this then? We gonna watch an X-rated movie?"

Charles allowed himself a gentle smile, and welcomed the slight relief in the atmosphere which this comment brought. He indicated the two chairs and they both sat.

"Matthew...may I call you Matthew?...Somewhat unusually, your late father, rather than commit his Last Will and Testament to paper in the normal way decided, instead, to record his wishes on cine film."

Matthew raised an eyebrow. "Ok. Is it legal to do that?"

"Oh yes. So long as certain statutory wording is used to ensure that the correct protocol is followed, and provided that one's wishes are clear, there shouldn't be any problem."

"Fine."

"Shall we begin?"

He waved a hand in a rather dismissive fashion.

"Please do."

Whilst trying to maintain his external air of cool professional-ism, now that the big moment had arrived Charles was feeling very excited. This was going to be very different to the norm and he just couldn't wait to see how Matthew was going to respond to what he was about to see. He signalled to James, who nodded and switched off the lights. Then he pushed a button on the projector; a soft whirring sound was heard and the film began to roll.

5

The first thing to be seen was simply an empty room - the one which Charles now knew to be the octagonal chamber in the tower. After a moment, the figure of Lord Alfred, looking surprisingly well, moved into the frame and sat down at his desk. He appeared so jaunty and full of excitement that it could only be supposed that he had made this film quite some time before his death. He was wearing a tailored smoking jacket of blue velvet - not that he ever smoked, of course, but Charles knew he felt such a garment to be part of the quintessentially British character that he had made his own. He regarded his audience, gazing directly into the camera lens for a long moment. Then he began:

"So, I suppose you'll finally be very happy to know that I am no longer resident in this world. And, I suppose, you're so absolutely stricken with grief that you're not even remotely concerned as to what little nest egg might be waiting for you from the - ahem - modest estate which I am fortunate enough to have built up. Well, more of that in a moment."

He paused for a second. Then his gaze hardened as he continued: "Now then, Matthew!"

Charles was sure the man physically jumped a little as his name was called.

"Your whole life has been characterised by wastefulness. Over and over again you have wasted your own money on countless pea-brained schemes and then you've come running to me for help to bail you out of your ever-increasing messes."

His tone softened a little as he continued. "I tried so hard to teach you all I could; I tried to instil in you the noble character which has been associated with the Willoughby name for generations. Was it asking too much to want my son to be a fine upstanding citizen?" An undercurrent of annoyance became apparent in his voice as he added, "I'd love to be standing there right now to ask you what you think of such an impressive record of - achievement."

Matthew scowled and sank a little lower in his chair.

"Now, my loyal butler, James."

Since this was, for James, the second viewing of the film he knew what was coming, but years of service caused him to instinctively draw himself fully upright and listen to his master attentively.

"You have served me well. There have been many times when I needed someone to rely on and, time and time again, you were that person. You have my heartfelt thanks."

"And Charles, my...so-" Lord Alfred paused, and seemed to have a moment's difficulty in breathing. Recovering swiftly, he looked back into the camera and continued, "...my solicitor. I have always been impressed with the standards you have exhibited in your work. All necessary details have always been attended to and," he paused again and gave a slight smile, "you have displayed great patience in your dealings with a grouchy old man."

Charles was aware that Matthew was becoming a little restless. The killer punch was almost upon them. Just stay calm, he told himself. You're an experienced solicitor. You know how to handle these situations, and you've faced more difficult ones than this. Remain cool and collected.

"And now," His Lordship continued, "we finally come to the moment you've all been waiting for - the division of the loot!"

"About time," grumbled Matthew, under his breath.

"So, let's make it all official then. Here goes."

He paused again, before clearing his throat very deliberately and taking a deep breath.

"I, Alfred Clifton Leonard Willoughby currently of Heston Grange, being of sound mind and body, do hereby make known my Last Will and Testament and, in so doing, hereby revoke all previous testamentary dispositions. And, just in case any of you should doubt my sanity," - he held up a piece of paper - "this is a letter signed by my doctor stating that I am perfectly well and in complete possession of all my faculties."

He glanced at it briefly.

"In fact, he even goes so far as to say that I am in surprisingly good shape for someone so advanced in years. I'm sure this knowledge is of great comfort to you, Matthew."

There was no mistaking the sarcasm in his voice. You could have heard a pin drop.

"Turning my attention to James first. I know that you have had to deal with some very difficult issues on a personal level and, although you have had to wrestle with your conscience on many occasions, I want you to know that I admire the way in which you have handled these various trials. At every stage you have displayed a level of integrity to which many others would do well to aspire."

James shuffled his feet a little and felt slightly awkward.

"I have therefore made arrangements that, on my death, the sum of five million pounds will be automatically transferred to your bank account. I sincerely hope this will be helpful as you continue to work through the circumstances facing you."

There was another pause. Lord Alfred sat, elbows on his antique writing desk, with chin resting on his upward-pointing fingertips. When he spoke again his voice had a more sombre tone, and had his eyes become just a little glazed?

"I will make no secret of my feelings on this matter: Matthew, my son, despite my highest hopes for you there have been many occasions when you have disappointed me. Yet, I cannot ignore the fact that, come fair wind or foul, you are still part of my family and, even now, I still hope and pray that you will become the fine fellow I always dreamed you to be."

Matthew seemed to visibly relax a little.

"At the same time, I am anxious to do what I can to ensure that my worldly wealth, being of no use to me anymore, is used in a sensible and responsible manner. Therefore, I am making one final and possibly futile attempt to get you to realise the importance of applying yourself to a task and carrying it through to completion. Somehow, I have to make you aware of the rewards that may be won or lost due to your success or failure to do so. And, to that end, I have decided to set a little challenge for you."

Matthew was now on the edge of his seat. So was Charles. The fact that he had already viewed the film in no way detracted from the drama of the situation.

"And, whilst this may come as something of a surprise, I have decided to include you, Charles, in this challenge - that is, if you would like to be involved. I feel that the exemplary quality of your service to me is deserving of some form of...how shall I put it?...acknowledgement."

He gave a little chuckle.

"In essence, it's really very simple," Lord Alfred continued, "I am about to go and hide this little trinket somewhere on the premises."

He produced from his pocket a small jewellery box which he turned to face the camera. Slowly, he opened the hinged lid to reveal a large, deep blue sapphire which sparkled as he carefully rotated the box in such a way as to ensure that the light reflected and glinted appealingly from its many expertly-crafted facets. The jewel was truly beautiful. Matthew tried to stifle a gasp, but both Charles and James heard him. It was almost as if the figure on the screen had heard too.

"You recognise this, my dear Matthew? Of course you do. It's the sapphire that you said you were going to buy for your dear mother's birthday back in the days when you had some money. As I recall, you decided instead to spend the money on a holiday for you and one of your many girlfriends. I wonder how long she stayed around? Well, no matter. Anyway, as you can see, I bought it instead, and now I'm going to hide it. And now we get to the part that will interest you."

He leaned forward and spoke carefully and slowly, almost conspiratorially.

"Matthew, my son, and Charles, my solicitor, this is a contest. Together with this little gem I will leave all the necessary information explaining how to affect the transfer of my estate to whichever one of you discovers it. With the exception of James' five million, find the sapphire and inherit the lot. But there's nothing in this game for coming second. Absolutely nothing. The winner takes all."

He smiled and waited a moment to allow his words to sink in. He let loose a hoarse cackle as he resumed:

"So I imagine you're probably already wondering where its hiding place could possibly be. Well, I'll tell you: *anywhere*. It could be anywhere in the environs of Heston Grange. Absolutely anywhere. In fact, the words 'needle' and 'haystack' come to mind. But, since you know me to be such a benevolent old fellow, I'm going to introduce a little culture to the proceedings by giving you a piece of poetry to assist you in your search. This is one of my favourite poems and I'm really rather proud of this. Are you sitting comfortably? Then listen, my dears; listen very, very carefully."

He was obviously relishing this whole presentation.

"The poem is as follows."

He cleared his throat and began.

'Like burnt-out torches by a sick man's bed
Gaunt cypress-trees stand round the sun bleached stone;
Here doth the little night-owl make her throne,
And the slight lizard show his jewelled head.
And, where the chaliced poppies flame to red,
In the still chamber of yon pyramid
Surely some Old-World Sphinx lurks darkly hid,
Grim warder of this pleasance of the dead.'"

In another life the old chap would have made a good actor; he had read very well.

"Suitably enigmatic, wouldn't you say? So there you have it, my dears. Pay close attention to all my words and, if you have the intelligence to work it out, these cryptic lines will lead you to the location of this all-important little blue stone." He held it up once again. "And, to be fair, the clues are not really that difficult; I'm sure you will see through them eventually." He chuckled again. "Well, I think that covers everything - oh, my mistake, there is one thing more; I almost forgot. You see, I couldn't resist putting just a small sting in the tail, so this little game of mine also carries a time limit. If neither of you have been able to discover the whereabouts of the sapphire exactly two weeks from the date of my demise, then my instructions are that my entire estate is to be sold and the proceeds shared equally between the Federation of British Artists and the Society of West End Theatre. There now, that's given you some food for thought hasn't it? You do remember what 'thought' is, Matthew? Who knows, maybe you're about to finally give some attention to your poor old dad's words of wisdom. Anyway, I'd love to stay and chat but I have to go and initiate a rather intriguing game of Hide and Seek. Thank you for your kind attention. Goodbye."

He rose from his seat, held the jewel before the camera one last time then, dropping it back into his pocket and giving a final cheeky smile to his audience, walked out of the frame in the same direction from which he had entered it. The film ended. The screen went dark and James began to open the curtains.

Other than the sound of the curtains gliding along their smooth rails the room was silent. The words of the poem rang in Charles' mind and he thought back to the night of Lord Alfred's death. With his final breath His Lordship had mentioned these cryptic lines. Charles hadn't known what he meant then but he did now, and cryptic they certainly were. Not surprisingly, Charles was now thoroughly intrigued as to exactly where the clues hidden within these lines would lead. How crafty Lord Alfred had been to devise such a scheme! And where was that large sapphire hidden? His thoughts were suddenly jolted back into the present as he became aware that Matthew was breathing loudly and deeply.

"That old bugger always had it in for me," he snarled.

6

What followed was an awkward quietness in the room which was suddenly shattered as Matthew leapt to his feet, knocking over the side table as he did so, on which stood the remains of his glass of sherry. As it hit the floor the delicate glass shattered, and the expensive carpet was spattered with the dark liquid and shards of broken glass. Ignoring the looks of surprise on the faces of the other two men, he stomped across the room with a face as dark as thunder, threw open the door and stormed out, slamming the door behind him, and leaving Charles and James momentarily stunned. He passed briskly along the numerous twisting corridors, eventually reaching the main entrance hall with its elaborate chandelier, and then out into the courtyard and the clear, crisp morning air. He walked up to his silver cobra, cursing under his breath and, as the frustration rose within him, he clenched his fist and brought it down firmly onto the bonnet. Why? he wondered. Why? Why? He should now be the proud possessor of a vast fortune. Instead, he found that he was having to play some ludicrous game - a game which he could quite possibly lose and end up with nothing! Was his father even allowed to do things this way, he wondered. He realised he already knew the answer. Whatever else he might think about his now deceased dad, there was one thing he would say for him - he was meticulous and thorough in whatever he put his hand to.

Just then, a thought struck him. In the film, the poem had mentioned something about a sun-bleached stone. Could that possibly be referring to the small disused family graveyard in the grounds? If that was where the sapphire was hidden Matthew was going to go and fetch it right now and bring this stupid farce of a contest to a swift conclusion. Without wasting a second, he turned on his heel and ran out of the courtyard, disappeared round the corner of the house and moved rapidly into the gardens beyond, in the direction of the cemetery.

"James, I'm so sorry," said Charles. "I had no idea his reaction would be quite so violent."

Having cleared away the pieces of broken glass, James had removed his jacket and was now on his hands and knees trying to sponge the sherry stain from the carpet.

"Oh, that's alright, sir. I think we both knew that master Matthew was hoping to hear something slightly different."

Charles' brow furrowed, and he asked, "James, naturally I am very excited at having been included in his Lordship's Will, but why? Why me?"

"Sir?"

"Why would he create a situation in which the very larger part of his estate could come to me, of all people?"

James paused in his cleaning and looked up. With a firm gaze he said,

"Lord Alfred held you in very high regard, sir, and, with all due respect, there isn't really anyone else living to whom he could have made such a gesture." He lowered his head and resumed his scrubbing.

Still marvelling at this remarkable turn of events, Charles picked up his legal pad and began to play the film again. Since the curtains where now open, the image on the screen was not so clear. However, this time he did not need to see, only to listen; and, when the words of the poem were recited, he began to write them down. Since his speed at shorthand was decidedly rusty, he needed to hear four further recitations to make sure he had the words written correctly. Then he sat in silence, reading them over and over. What could they mean? Then it occurred to him that he did not even know what a cypress tree looked like. Perhaps he needed to find out? A quick scan of the library shelves enabled him to find a large illustrated dictionary; and he was interested to discover that as well as being the name of a tree, the word 'cypress' also described a type of thin black fabric, often associated with funerals.

Almost out of breath, Matthew shoved open the small wooden gate, set into a fragile-looking fence with flaking white paint, and lurched into the cemetery. As he entered, the sounds of the crashing waves from the nearby ocean receded. No birds sang here, and the wind respectfully kept its distance. This quiet haven lay virtually hidden from view, being bordered on three sides by a combination of tall hedges and coniferous trees. The cemetery itself, though, was in a state of disrepair. What had once been well kept foliage and neat topiary was now messy and unkempt. Piles of old dry leaves were everywhere covering the ground, along with a mass of poison ivy, whose creeping branches threatened to trip up all but the most careful of visitors. The last interring had occurred long before Lord and Lady Willoughby had moved into Heston Grange and many of the inscriptions on the gravestones had now all but worn away through constant exposure to the elements.

Glancing this way and that, Matthew's attention was drawn to the memorial at the far end of the grave site. Standing apart from the others, and on its own plinth, this one must have been in honour of an owner of Heston Grange who was especially esteemed. In its prime it would have looked immaculate, with all kinds of ornate carving in the stonework round the sides, but now it was rather weather beaten, and a number of weeds grew around its base. Its top was a flat piece of white marble and - Matthew suddenly noticed - it was directly beneath two overhanging trees. He didn't really know anything about different varieties of tree but, he wondered, could these be the cypress trees mentioned in the poem? He began to examine the grave closely, circling it and looking for anything that might provide some sort of further clue. What he really needed, he realised, was to go back to the house and write down the words of that blasted poem. He was just turning to leave when he noticed, near the base of the plinth on which the memorial stood, that one of the pieces of stone seemed to be a little out of alignment. Crouching down, he also found that its position exposed an edge which appeared unsullied by the ravages of time. Had this stone been moved recently? He reached out and pushed it. It was loose! Getting down on his knees and bringing both hands to bear on the stone, he managed to loosen it further, creating a gap into which he could slide his fingers. He was then able to grasp the stone and, little by little, he worked it backwards until, all at once, the whole stone slid out, revealing the dark cavity behind. The opening was only just large enough for Matthew to thread his hand inside. His wrist and forearm became grazed on the surrounding stonework as he groped about, feeling for - for what? He didn't know, but hoped it would be obvious if he did manage to discover anything. His searching fingertips were just finding damp earth and he would feel an occasional tickle as some insect or other scurried across the back of his hand. Then, suddenly, he felt an object that was far too geometrically defined to be found naturally in such a location. Gently taking hold of it, he carefully eased both it and his hand back through the opening in the memorial and brought his find out into the light of day. It was a small grey metal box with a hinged lid. When he saw it, Matthew gasped in surprise and felt his pulse quicken. He recognised the box as being one that his father used to keep in his study. Slowly and deliberately, he moved away from the grave and sat down against one of the overhanging trees. Holding the box in front of him, he took a deep breath and slowly opened the lid.

It took him a moment to register what he saw. According to the film, it was a blue sapphire that his father was going to hide, so what was this red jewel doing here? He picked it up but then realised

immediately that it was nothing but a plastic imitation. Then he noticed the piece of paper which had been lying beneath it. Taking it
from the box and unfolding it, he read, *"You didn't really think I'd make
it that easy, did you? Ha ha!"* Matthew cursed and threw the worthless
gem into the bushes.

Meanwhile, Charles was still in the library, reading and re-reading
the words of the poem. What was he trying to find? What was he looking for? He hadn't any idea. He watched the film yet again. Still no
luck. Lord Alfred's words seemed to mock him from the screen. *"The
clues are not really that difficult; I'm sure you will see through them eventually."* Well, Charles certainly hadn't seen through these 'easy' clues
up to now. He stood up and placed the poem carefully in his pocket.
Glancing down at the still damp patch on the carpet it seemed that
James had made a pretty good job of removing the stain. Once it was
dry you would probably never know there had been a spillage at all.
  He walked out into the corridor, and paused looking in both directions. As he took in the large number of doors along this corridor
alone he began to realise the potential magnitude of the task that he
was facing. How many other corridors did this crumbling old mansion contain? Charles wasn't sure, but he knew it was a lot; and the lack
of regular symmetrical design didn't help either. Anyone, throughout
the whole of history, who had ever wanted to hide anything, could not
have chosen a better hiding place than Heston Grange. Being in want
of any sort of idea as to what this cryptic poem might mean, Charles
walked off into the maze of corridors in the hope that some sort of
inspiration might strike.

Matthew ran back into the entrance hall, now totally furious. He
made straight for the nearest closed door, wrestled it open and
stomped into the room beyond. Every item of furniture in the room
was covered with a dust sheet. He gave a cry of exasperation and began frantically pulling them off, one after another. Great clouds of
dust billowed enthusiastically into the air and span in his wake as he

worked his way round the room. He uncovered what turned out to be an antique writing bureau and immediately began pulling open all of its drawers, rifling through the contents without any thought as to whether they were important or carefully ordered. A single all-consuming passion filled his mind: Find that sapphire! Find it!

He paused in his search as he became aware of a shadowy figure standing in the doorway. James stepped fully into view as he entered the room. Matthew looked at the floor, feeling a little sheepish as he stood in the jumbled pile of papers now lying at his feet.

"Please don't worry about the mess, master Matthew. I'll tidy it up."

The habit of a lifetime of service ensured his tone remained civil. Matthew mumbled something that might have been half an apology and headed for the door. He was about to make his exit, but then he hesitated and turned back to see the elderly butler picking up all the dropped papers. He returned to him and joined in with the clear-up.

"You really don't need to trouble yourself, sir."

"That's alright, James. I'm sorry about all this. I...I've...well, today has just been a bit of a roller-coaster ride, that's all."

"I can well imagine, sir."

There followed a lull in the conversation as the tidying was done, although James sensed that their talking was not quite over, just yet. He was right.

"Er...James?"

"Yes, sir?"

"Why did my father hate me so much?"

What a question. James paused, the half-sorted documents in his hands temporarily forgotten. There was an appreciable silence before he spoke, and his tone was kind.

"Your father always maintained the highest hopes for you, sir."

He immediately returned to his task and Matthew realised that this particular conversation was over, at least for now.

Later, as shadows lengthened and the sun began to set once more, Charles, with his mission anything but accomplished, re-emerged from the depths of Heston Grange into the more frequented areas of the house; and, in due course, came and sat in the dining room at a long wooden table, which could have accommodated twenty people quite comfortably, and awaited the arrival of one of Mrs Gillcarey's delicious home-cooked dinners. He had made a point of ensuring that two places should be set, although whether Matthew would actually appear and join his new rival for the meal was perhaps another question. At the far end of the room a large fire blazed cheerfully in the hearth around which two Chesterfield sofas and several high backed chairs were arranged.

Charles sighed and gazed at his distorted reflection in the base of the silver candelabrum that stood on the table, with a tiny, tapering flame atop each of its deep red candles. For a moment his thoughts drifted back to the moment when he finally realised he was no longer engaged. Maybe he had been neglectful in some way? Certainly, having never known his own father he felt to some extent that he was having to navigate uncharted waters without a guide, as it were. But why? The question boomed and reverberated through his mind. Why had she left him? Everything had seemed to be going so well...

His reverie was interrupted by the sound of the dining room door opening. He glanced up, expecting to see Mrs Gillcarey make her entrance but it was, in fact, a rather crestfallen Matthew who came in. They made eye contact and Charles gave a slight nod. Matthew stayed where he was and looked at the floor. After a few moments he looked up and said, quietly, "Erm...may I join you?"

Charles smiled and indicated the vacant seat at the table.

He slowly made his way across the room and sat down.

"Would you care for a glass of wine?"

Charles held up a bottle of a particularly fine Barollo, rich and full bodied, which James had uncorked some thirty minutes ago to allow it to breathe. Matthew managed a slight smile and held out his glass. The crackling fire in the hearth, the flickering candles and the beautifully delicate sound of the vintage wine as it left its bottle and softly splashed into the cut crystal glass would have made a perfect moment in other circumstances. They clinked their glasses and sipped in silence, savouring the smooth, fruity liquid as its palette of flavours broke over their tongues. Matthew cleared his throat.

"Er...Mr Seymour, I owe you an apology."

"You do?"

"Well, yes. My outburst earlier on was quite uncalled for. It won't happen again."

"No need for an apology, Mr Willoughby, but since you have offered it, it would be most un-gentlemanly of me not to accept."

"That film was...well...it just gave me a bit of a shock."

"To be quite honest with you, I'm not surprised."

"You see, the thing is..."

He stopped speaking as the door opened and James entered. He walked over to the dumb waiter, slid open the door and, reaching inside, began to pull on the ropes.

Some distance below stairs a beautifully cooked leg of roast venison began to ascend from Mrs Gillcarey's kitchen, its delicious aroma sufficient to win over even the most fastidious of vegetarians. On arrival, James lifted the silver platter with its steaming joint from the hatch and carried it to the table. Setting it down precisely, with practised ease he proceeded to carve several slices, all uniformly thick. By the time he had added the garlic mash and roast potatoes, chipolatas, mange tout, carrots, peas, sage and chestnut stuffing and a generous helping of Mrs Gillcarey's rich onion gravy, made according to her secret recipe, the meal had become a veritable work of art.

"Thank you, James," said Charles. "This looks magnificent! Please pass our thanks to Mrs Gillcarey."

He nodded. "Very good, sir."

He turned and left the two men to enjoy the meal, the presentation of which was surpassed only by its taste. They both ate with enthusiasm. Old Lord Alfred was clearly accustomed to doing himself well, and he had managed to find the perfect housekeeper in Mrs Gillcarey.

After the meal, they adjourned to the armchairs in front of the fire, where they sat for a while, just staring into the flames. Then, as he refilled their glasses, yet again, with the ruby coloured wine, Charles spoke.

"You were saying..?"

"Sorry?"

"Just before James came in to serve dinner, you were about to tell me something."

Matthew paused and set down his glass.

"Yes. I just wanted to explain..." His voice tailed off and his fingers fumbled against each other as he sought to find the right words.

Then, all at once, he suddenly seemed to find his stride.

"When I was growing up, I so desperately wanted to be like my father. He was so successful, admired and respected by everyone."

"There's nothing wrong with that. Plenty of boys want to be like Dad."

"Yes, only it seemed that whatever I did to try and impress him was never good enough. Trying to get praise out of him was like trying to get blood out of a stone. But at the same time, he would be openly critical of anything I did that was even slightly imperfect, pouring scorn on everything - even in front of other people."

Charles eyed Matthew as he poured out his heart and soul and felt a pang of sympathy for him. How could he feel otherwise? His mother had raised him by herself and flatly refused to discuss his father on those occasions when Charles had been brave enough to broach the subject. "You have me," she used to snap, "and I'm all you need."

"On top of that," Matthew continued, "whether I was just imagining it I don't know, but it seemed to me that all my friends got on with their dads really well. And no matter what I tried to do..." he faltered and looked down. "I...I just found that it was difficult to talk to him about things that mattered to me; and a sort of void developed, an empty hollow. And now he's gone...and I...I can't help feeling as though there's a piece of the puzzle missing."

In his professional capacity, Charles had heard variations on this theme time and time again. Was it preferable, he wondered for the hundredth time, to not have a father at all, as in his case, or to have a father - but one who did not display the affection and acceptance which every boy needs? A pointless question, he concluded, since no-one can change their situation in that regard. They just have to soldier on and make the best of it, with whatever hand they've been dealt. But he was starting to see the young man from a different perspective, he realised.

"And now," he continued, morosely, "with all this farcical business of having to solve the clues or inherit nothing...I just feel like it's one last kick in the teeth."

Just then, James entered carrying a tray, bearing a decanter of tawny port and two glasses. He placed a glass of the nectar in front of both Charles and Matthew then moved to the table and began to clear away the remains of the dinner. During this pause in the conversation Charles ran through the extraordinary events of the last few days in his mind and silently reached a moment of decision; he leant forward in his chair and said, "Matthew, I have an idea."

"Oh?" Matthew raised his head from his despondent thoughts.

"Well, I can assure you that I have been just as surprised as you to find out what your father had to say concerning each of us, although obviously for different reasons. Now then, rather than be at loggerheads with each other over this, why don't we join forces?"

"I don't quite follow."

"We could team up; figure out the clues and solve them together; and, instead of one winner taking everything, we could both be winners and take half each."

Matthew didn't say anything but was obviously considering it. Certainly, he thought, his efforts so far had proved entirely fruitless and, realistically, what chance would he, of all people, have against the logical and clear thinking mind of a solicitor?

"And," Charles continued, "if we work together on this, it would increase our chances of solving the conundrum before the deadline is reached, after which neither of us will get anything."

"Good point."

"Ahem." James had cleared the table and approached. "Will there be anything else, gentlemen?"

"No thanks, James. That will be all."

"Thank you, sir. Goodnight, sirs."

With a curt nod he turned and left, gently closing the door behind him.

There was a pause.

Charles spoke first. "Well..?"

Matthew thought for a moment longer. Then he smiled and stood up. "Mr Seymour, you have a deal."

Charles now stood too. Silhouetted against the light from the dying embers, the two men shook hands.

7

The next day, as Charles was making the lengthy hike from his bedroom down to the morning room for breakfast, he happened to almost bump into James as he appeared suddenly from a side corridor.

"Oh! James! Good morning. You startled me."

"I'm very sorry, sir; that was not my intention."

"That's ok. I'm just coming down for some breakfast. Has Matthew surfaced yet?"

"Yes, sir. Master Matthew has already started his breakfast."

"Right, so it seems that I have some catching up to do then, eh?"

There was a momentary pause that felt decidedly awkward, after which James said, "Sir...if I may?"

"Yes, of course. What is it?"

The butler looked up and down the corridor to make sure they were not being overheard and then spoke again, his voice little more than a whisper.

"May I speak frankly, sir?"

"Please do."

"Thank you, sir. In one sense, the division of His Lordship's estate is none of my business. By the terms of the Will I have come into a very substantial sum and perhaps I should just let my involvement end there." He paused. Charles' eyes narrowed.

"Then why don't you?"

"Well, sir, I couldn't help overhearing some of your conversation with master Matthew last night and the...the arrangement which the two of you have now entered into."

"Well, that's alright, James. I know you to be a discreet fellow; it doesn't matter to me in the slightest that you know what our plans are."

"Of course, sir. What I'm trying to say is...well...please be careful, sir. As I've mentioned to you before, although it grieves me to say it, master Matthew is... he's a scoundrel, sir. His father was right to be very careful in his dealings with him."

"James, I appreciate your kind concern, but I've had a long talk with Matthew. He's a decent chap really - he's just been misunderstood, that's all. Anyway, now that we've agreed to go halves on everything he'll have every incentive to really work with me, not against me."

James looked down and pursed his lips.

"Very well, sir. Whatever you think is best. I apologise if I have in any way spoken out of turn."

"Not at all. I'm greatly encouraged that you would voice your concerns like this. Now, I need to get some breakfast."

James watched as Charles walked away and disappeared round the corner at the end of the corridor.

"Do be careful," he muttered under his breath. "Master Matthew is a scoundrel."

He turned and walked away to attend to his duties, still muttering to himself. "A scoundrel indeed."

Mrs Gillcarey looked after both Charles and Matthew wonderfully. After the hearty breakfast (during which Charles thought several times that he would have no hope at all of attracting a member of the fairer sex if he continued to add to his waistline like this) the two riddle-solvers sat in the morning room, with large mugs of steaming freshly ground Colombian coffee, going over the words of the cryptic lines again.

Like burnt out torches by a sick man's bed

"Might that be referring to Dad's actual bed?" wondered Matthew, aloud. "It seems that he was pretty sick by the end."

"Possibly," Charles replied, "but how does that tie in with the next line?"

Gaunt cypress-trees stand round the sun-bleached stone

"I did think, yesterday, that perhaps it might be referring to the private cemetery in the grounds so I went to have a look at it."

"And...?"

"Didn't find anything." Charles nodded, unaware of the half-truth of this statement.

Quickly, Matthew said, "The actual choice of words seems very flowery for Dad."

Charles' mouth fell open in surprise.

"Of course! That must be it!"

"Must be what?"

"Matthew, you're a genius! I've been acting on the assumption that your father wrote this poem himself but, given the style of the writing, I think there's a good chance we might just find it on one of the shelves in the library. Come on!"

They walked briskly from the room in search of Lord Alfred's poetry collection.

After this burst of euphoria the actual locating of the poem proved to be a more difficult task than either man would have liked. They pulled volume after volume from the shelves, scouring the contents page of each one, and then the index of first lines. The stack of discarded books grew larger as the number of items remaining on the shelves grew fewer. Time ticked by and the minutes became hours. At length, Matthew picked up a volume by Alfred Lord Tennyson.

"I suppose it would be far too obvious for Dad to make use of the Lord Alfred/Alfred Lord connection?" he wondered aloud.

Charles chuckled. "Good thinking. It might be worth examining it extra closely, just to be on the safe side."

Matthew gave a sigh and began to turn the pages.

It was some considerable time later, not long after James had brought in yet another pot of Earl Grey tea with some generous slices of Dundee cake, that Charles gave a startled yelp. Matthew looked up from the weighty Tennyson volume in his hands.

"You found something?" he asked.

Charles nodded, letting the collection of Wilfred Owen poetry drop to the floor beside him. "Maybe. I do hope so."

"Well?"

"It's something that Lord Alfred said in the film. *This is one of my favourite poems,*"

"Yes...so?"

"Look."

Charles slowly raised his hand and pointed to a high shelf on which sat a single volume, bound in red leather with gold block lettering on its spine. The title read, "My Favourite Poems."

Matthew was already out of his seat and reaching up to pull the dusty book from the shelf. Excitedly, they sat shoulder to shoulder and opened it. As the book fell open the gilt-edged pages revealed that this was no ordinary volume. Originally, a long time ago, the pages had all been blank. Now, however, there was a handwritten poem on each one, and each was presented in Lord Alfred's very best calligraphy.

"Well, well," said Charles, "maybe he did write the poem himself after all."

The script was cursive and contained many illuminated letters, expertly and artistically crafted. Shapes and colours all blended so effectively and, Charles noticed, enhanced the mood which the words of the poem were trying to convey. Matthew was in awe.

"I knew he was a keen artist," he whispered, "but these are amazing."

Charles could only agree. Reverently, he turned the fragile pages but stopped when he came to the page which contained the now familiar cryptic lines. They both stared at it.

"Well, there it is. So what now?"

"Might it be that this particular version of the poem contains some clue or other that we wouldn't notice if we just studied the text in our own handwriting?"

"Possibly, but what can it be?"

There was so much detail in these masterpieces. Who could say where a clue might be cunningly concealed? Perhaps they would need to locate a magnifying glass.

Just then, James entered to announce that luncheon was served.

A few minutes later found the two self-styled sleuths entering the conservatory. It was a large summery room, whose French windows and open patio doors welcomed plenty of daylight. Wicker furniture and comfortable cushions added to the relaxed ambience. Charles momentarily marvelled that such a charming room could be found at all in a house which seemed to exist in such a state of perpetual darkness.

Against one wall was an aquarium in which swam all manner of tropical fish. Charles was no expert where fish were concerned but he did recognise some rainbow fish, a few guppies, a catfish and even a bright orange oscar fish with its ostentatious tail.

As they settled themselves at the table Mrs Gillcarey came bustling in and began to carve some succulent ham. There was also a home baked loaf of bread, still warm from the oven, and a large bowl of waldorf salad. Fresh mango juice was poured into tall glasses. As they began to eat, Mrs Gillcarey spoke.

"Begging your pardon, gentlemen." They looked up. "Tomorrow is the day when the window cleaners are booked to come. I was just wondering whether I should put them off for the time being?"

Charles and Matthew looked at each other and shrugged.

"I don't think that'll be a problem," said Charles. "I can't see how they will get in our way. They might as well still come."

"Very good, sir. As my mother used to say - God rest her - there's nothing quite so unpleasant as dirty windows; and now I've inherited her feelings on the matter!" She curtsied politely before scurrying away to finish preparing one of her 'specialities', which later turned out to be a perfect bread pudding with thick Devon custard - the ultimate comfort food. She produced it with pride, though blushed with pleasure at the diners' effusive compliments.

As they completed the meal, Matthew said, "In the absence of any other ideas, perhaps we should examine the hand-written poem again in tandem with having another look at the film."

Charles agreed and they returned to the library. Once there, while he waited for Matthew to start the projector, Charles began to flick through the pages looking for the poem, but then cried out in surprise.

"What is it?" asked Matthew.

"Well," he replied, "this just becomes more and more curious."

Holding the book out to Matthew, he pointed to the poem but then turned the page...and there was the same poem written out again. True, some of the lettering was slightly different - not surprising in handwriting of this style - and the second version had been written a little further down the page for some reason, but the text was identical. They flicked the pages back and forth a few times.

"Now, why would Dad go to all the trouble of writing out the same poem twice, on opposite sides of the same sheet of paper?" said Matthew.

"Beats me," Charles replied. "Let's watch the film."

Matthew set it running and they watched, yet again. They saw Lord Alfred make his entrance; they saw him reward James, rebuke Matthew and commend Charles; they watched as he held the sapphire aloft and recited that wretched poem; and then -

"Wait!" shouted Charles. "Wind the film back. I want to hear that bit again."

Matthew did so. Something was trying to surface in Charles' mind.

Mrs Gillcarey dislikes being unable to see through dirty windows.

The film was running again.

"...the clues are not that difficult. I am sure you will see through them eventually."

On impulse, he snatched up the book and folded it right back on itself so the crucial page stood out alone. Moving over to the large bay window he held it up to the bright sunlight. At first, he couldn't quite make sense of the jumble of ornate letters; but then, suddenly, he saw it.

"Well, I'll be!"

"What is it?" asked Matthew, joining him in the window. "What have you found?"

"Well, take a look for yourself."

At first, Matthew also didn't know what he was looking for but then, all at once, he saw it too.

What he saw appeared to be some sort of architectural plan. Then, recognition dawned and, once again, he found himself marvelling at his late father's ingenuity. Incredibly, with the light shining through the page, the elaborate lettering of the two versions of the poem combined to form an outline-plan of Heston Grange! True, not every room was shown, but there was the main front door, here was the entrance hall, and here were all those warren-like corridors. And then, as they continued to stare at it in amazement, it was Matthew who found what really mattered.

"Look!" he exclaimed. "There!"

Jabbing his finger at the page there appeared to be a small red 'x' in a room adjacent to one of the turrets.

"Well," said Charles, his feelings of excitement covered with traditional British reserve, "I suggest we make that location our next destination."

Taking the all-important book with them, they sprinted from the library and out into the maze of corridors.

8

Sometimes running, sometimes walking briskly, Charles and Matthew turned left and right through the endless maze of passageways which was Heston Grange. Although they had Lord Alfred's hand-drawn map to guide them it was difficult to follow it at times, since it was hardly of Ordnance Survey standard, and their route passed through some dark areas of the irregularly shaped house where was no light source to enable them to look at it properly. Added to that was the realisation that there was no indication as to which floor the red X referred to. All they knew for sure was that it had been marked next to one of the manor's turrets. After what seemed an age of scurrying this way and that, upstairs and down, Matthew, who had been leading the way with the book in hand, came to a stop. They were now on the top floor and Charles, catching up a moment later, was somewhat out of breath, thanks to all the stairs. Matthew examined the map again.

"Well," he began, "if I'm reading this correctly the room we're after is on the other side of this wall."

"So where's the way in?"

There was no door; just oak panelling. But this panelling was slightly different to elsewhere in the house because many years ago a craftsman had engraved into the wood, and then painted, posy of red poppies.

Reasoning that the entrance must be round the other side they immediately tried to get there, but it proved not to be as simple as just walking round the corner. There appeared to be no direct route. Once again they had to brave the catacomb-like structure of the house. Eventually, though, Matthew once again halted - by another wall. Again, no door.

"Do you suppose it could be a secret room?" wondered Charles, "A bit like the octagonal room in the tower - completely enclosed. No windows, and impossible to detect because of the ramshackle layout of the place."

"Damn!" Matthew slammed his fist against the oak panelling. "How are we supposed to get in?"

"Stay calm. If there is a room behind here I'm sure Lord Alfred would have ensured it was possible for us to get in."

Charles began to run his fingertips over the rough, gnarled oak panelling. It was difficult to see anything clearly with what little light managed to find its way into the area.

"Shall I fetch a torch?"

"Good idea. In the meantime I'll keep searching."

"For what, exactly?"

"Well, if I find it I'll tell you."

Matthew vanished into the gloom on his quest for some illumination. Left alone, Charles continued to explore the panelling. Surely there must be some sort of doorway?

Suddenly, he froze. He had heard something. It was similar to the sound he'd heard in the library a couple of days ago. There it was again. That same scrabbling sound. James had thought it might be a rat. It didn't sound like a rat to Charles. He moved back into the shadows as he realised that someone was moving along one of the corridors in his direction. It was probably James, he told himself, yet his heart pounded with the feeling that something was not quite right. Should he stay concealed or confront this mysterious stranger? Before he had any more time to think a shape materialised out of the darkness and, before he quite knew what he was doing, he had stepped out in front of it.

The shape screamed and dropped a large stack of bed linen. "Oh, sir, you startled me!"

"Mrs Gillcarey, I'm so sorry." Charles stooped to help her pick up all the sheets and pillowcases, while she was clucking around like some old mother hen.

"Oh, that's alright, sir. My own silly fault, really. There now, no harm done." Tut-tutting to herself she gathered everything up. Then, with her arms full, she tried to blow the hair out of her eyes which had somehow fallen over her face in the excitement.

"I do apologise again, Mrs Gillcarey. It's just that I've been hearing some strange sounds during my stay at Heston Grange, and they have started to make me feel a little on edge."

Mrs Gillcarey laughed. It was a round, comfortable laugh.

"Ho ho ho. Well, Mr Seymour, sir, from time to time I have heard tales that this house has more than its fair share of spooks but you can take it from me that I've never seen any. No. Not even one. Anyway, if I did see something I think they'd probably be more frightened at the sight of me than the other way about!" She laughed again.

"Thank you, that's good to hear."

"Er...is there anything I can help you with, sir?"

"Well, actually, as a matter of fact, yes, perhaps you can help. I believe there may be a room on the other side of this wall. Would you happen to know anything about that?"

"Oh, certainly sir."

"You do?" Charles could hardly believe his ears.

"Yes, sir. There is a room behind there. It used to be occupied by Meg, the Lord and Lady's maid. She doesn't work here now though. After Lord Alfred lost his wife he felt he didn't need the services of a maid so she was let go. Still, she ain't done too badly out of it - His Lordship said she could stay in the Lodge, and that's where she's been from that day to this."

"How do I get into the room?"

"Through the door, sir." She spoke with a mischievous twinkle in her eye.

"Hmm...quite so, Mrs Gillcarey. Er...where is it?"

"Oh, there I go forgetting my place! I'm sorry, sir. I shouldn't waste your time by jesting, you being a busy man and all. The door's right here."

She stepped aside and pointed to a particular portion of panelling.

"That's it? That's the door?"

"Yes, sir. There's no handle, but you can see...just there...is a tiny keyhole."

Charles pushed against the panelling.

"It appears to be locked."

"Yes, sir, and the key has been missing for quite some time. No idea where it is."

"I suppose we could always just break it down."

"Oh, I wouldn't do that, sir. All this timber is very old. You start crashing and banging about, you're likely to bring the whole thing falling in."

Thinking back to the rickety bridge leading to the tower, Charles had to agree.

"Was there anything else, sir?"

"No, thank you. You've been very helpful."

She went on her way and was swallowed up by the darkness just as Matthew returned with a torch. Charles showed him the keyhole. It wasn't at all surprising that they had been unable to see it at first, hidden as it was positioned between two knots in the wood. Then he told him about his conversation with the Housekeeper and about Meg, the former maid.

"Well, she might be able to tell us where the key is," said Matthew, "and if she's just in the Lodge at the end of the drive perhaps we should pay her a little visit."

9

The afternoon had suddenly become much colder. Charles and Matthew walked down the long driveway towards the main gate and the lodge. They had considered using the car but decided the exercise would do them both good, having been cooped up inside for the last couple of days. It didn't occur to either of them that they had actually been getting plenty of exercise already as they worked their way all over the house in their search for clues. Furthermore, they hadn't quite realised just how far away the lodge was and now, as the wind picked up and the chill started to bite, they both privately wondered whether taking the car hadn't been such a bad idea after all. With collars turned up and hands thrust deeply into pockets they trudged along the unmetalled road and sighed with relief as the lodge at last came into view, with the high imposing gates to the outside world just beyond.

The lodge was a quaint, quintessentially English cottage with lattice windows. A white picket fence stood a few feet in front of it, with a gate opening onto a short pathway of crazy paving. This lead up to a panelled front door in which just one of the panels was made of glass, enabling the occupant to see who was visiting before opening the door. All the curtains were closed, but the glow from some lights within could be seen at their edges so Charles and Matthew approached the door and knocked. They waited for a few moments but there was no response. Matthew raised his fist to knock again, but just at that moment a small wrinkled face appeared in the glass panel and eyed them both. After pausing for only a moment, the head nodded in apparent satisfaction and disappeared, after which a bolt was drawn back and the door was opened. Charles stepped forward and offered his hand.

"Hello, my name is- "

"I'm glad you've finally arrived," she interrupted, sweetly. "I've been waiting for you. Come inside and I'll bring you your coffee."

Charles exchanged a puzzled glance with Matthew and, somewhat bemused, the two of them followed her in. She led the way into a small but comfortable sitting room containing sofas and chairs which were over stuffed, and ornaments of all kinds adorning shelves in every inch of available wall space. She motioned for them to be seated and then went through another door into her even smaller kitchen from where the sounds of cups and saucers rattling together could be heard, along with a kettle boiling. She came back a couple of minutes later carrying a tray.

"Here's your tea," she said. "Nice and hot, just the way you like it. Oh, now look at me! I forgot to bring any cake."

Before either man could speak, she beetled away and various kitchen-like sounds emanated once again. Returning a few moments later, she proudly announced, "Here we are, then. A nice selection of biscuits. Please help yourselves."

They began to sip their tea, and Matthew nibbled on a biscuit. Meg watched them attentively, a maternal smile on her tiny face, while Charles tried to think how to start the conversation. After a moment, he cleared his throat.

"Er...Meg?"

"You'll think me very foolish," she interjected, "but I can never remember which of you is which." She paused, obviously giving the matter some thought, before continuing. "No, it's no use. You'll just have to tell me." She gave an attractive little-old-lady giggle. "Which one of you is James?"

"Er...well actually, Meg, Neither of us is James. My name is Charles, and this is Matthew. We've come to ask you about your old room in the manor?"

No response.

"The one with the hidden door in the panelling?"

"Go easy on James," she said. Then she leaned forward and whispered, "He has alzheimer's, you know."

"Meg, I know it might be difficult for you to remember, but can you recall what happened to the key to your old room?"

"The key?"

"Yes. At the moment, the door is locked and we can't find the key. Can you think where it might be?"

"James was always such a nice fellow. He looked after me very well."

"Meg, do you know where the key is? We need to get into your old room. It's really very important."

"Is Mrs Gillcarey still there?"

"Meg, please!"

"Hmm?"

"Where is the key?"

"Oh yes, the key, yes. Erm...now let me see. Oh, I'm not sure I can remember. Which key do you mean?" She giggled again. "Oh, I know it must be round here somewhere."

Matthew, who was becoming increasingly impatient, stood up and walked over to a Welsh dresser that was really too large for this small room. With a glance in Charles' direction he began to open the drawers and started rummaging through them. Charles was both shocked and embarrassed and opened his mouth to say- he knew not what. But, since Meg didn't seem to mind this rather intrusive behaviour, he remained quiet. He sat and watched her as she sipped her tea, demurely, lifting both the cup and saucer in the way proper ladies would, while Matthew rifled through all those over-full drawers, as proper gentlemen wouldn't. Meg might not know where the key is, he thought, but it's just as unlikely that she would know where anything else is either, in all this jumble of ancient clutter.

"Aha!"

With a look of satisfaction, Matthew extracted a bunch of keys from one of the drawer's nethermost recesses and held them up. All manner of sizes, and some of them looked very old and rusty. He crossed to Meg, who was still staring impassively into her teacup.

"Meg, is one of these the key to your old room?"

She took the bunch in her delicate hand and, with a small sigh, gazed at the conglomeration before her.

Oh...yes, I think so...probably. But I can't remember which one it would be. No, wait...I think perhaps this one seems familiar."

She held up an iron key which was quite long and obviously old.

Gently, Charles said, "Thank you, Meg. You've been very helpful. Would it be alright if we took these keys away with us for a short time? We'll return them to you as soon as we have the door open."

She gave another of her small smiles and nodded. Matthew was already heading for the door. Charles paused and looked back.

"Thank you for the tea, Meg."

"You're welcome. Please ask James to come and see me. I do miss him so."

He nodded and left, quietly closing the front door behind him.

Meg sat for a long time after that, staring into the middle distance and continuing to sip her tea even after it had gone cold.

Charles had to run to catch up with Matthew who was already some distance along the driveway, holding the keys in his hand and heading towards the house with renewed determination.

"How could you do that?"

"Do what?"

"Just start picking through an old lady's personal things?"

"Come on, give me a break. It was obvious that she's senile; and it wasn't as though I was stealing from her."

"Still, I think you should have waited for her permission."

Matthew stopped walking and turned to face Charles. "Ok, you're right. You want me to take the keys back?"

Charles looked at the ground and felt awkward. "No, but-"

"Thought not." He started walking again, then turned to look back to where Charles was still standing. "Are you coming?"

Charles heaved a sigh of resignation and followed. The sky continued to darken as they approached the house and rumblings of thunder could be heard in the distance.

A few minutes later found the two of them back in the gloomy corridor outside the secret room. Charles held the torch while Matthew selected the key which Meg had pointed out. As he moved it towards the keyhole it was immediately apparent that it was far too large. In exasperation he tried one of the other keys, then another, and still another. None of them worked. Then he tried every one of them again, just in case. Despite his perseverance, however, the door remained decidedly locked. With a cry of frustration he gave the door a hefty kick. That didn't work either. Obviously angry now, he began to use some words that Charles hadn't heard before.

"Perhaps Meg might have some other keys?" he suggested, when he was able to get a word in.

"Yeah, maybe. Stupid old biddy."

"Shall we go back and ask her?"

"I suppose so."

As they left the house for the second time they found that the rain was now falling heavily and the thunder was louder. This time, they decided to take the car. Charles unlocked his Jaguar and they both climbed in. The engine roared and the vehicle pulled out of the courtyard.

"Oh, how lovely to see you again!" said Meg, as she answered the door. "It really doesn't seem like a week since you were last here. My goodness, doesn't time fly! Well, come in out of the rain and I'll put the kettle on."

"Actually, Meg," said Charles, calling after her as he followed her into the tiny hallway, "we don't really have time for tea on this occasion. What we really need is some more of your help."

"Oh?" She paused and turned back to face him. "Well, what can I do for you?"

Charles held up the keys.

"Oh, I was wondering where they had got to. Someone was asking about these quite recently."

He didn't bother to explain, but continued, "Meg, we still need the key to your old room in the manor. None of these fit the lock."

"But I did tell you, this is the one you need." She again indicated the old iron key.

"We've tried it, Meg. It doesn't work."

"Doesn't it? I'm sure it was alright the last time I used it."

Matthew was starting to get impatient again.

Charles shot him a glance. "Meg, do you have any other keys?"

"I don't think so. This is the one you need."

Now Charles was becoming frustrated too. "Meg, this key does not open the door to your room."

"I know that."

"What?" Matthew was incredulous. Charles was puzzled.

"I thought I'd explained it all to you...or maybe I didn't...ah well, I can't remember. Anyway, follow me."

As she turned away Matthew whispered, "We don't have time for this. Let's get back to the house. Maybe we can find some other clues in the map book or on the film."

"Down here." Meg was holding open a door which revealed a flight of wooden steps descending into a cellar.

"Let's humour her for a moment," said Charles, under his breath, "then we'll be on our way."

Meg reached inside the door, pulled a string and a low-wattage naked light bulb flickered into life. They followed her down the stairs into the low-ceilinged cellar filled with wooden packing cases.

"These are all my things that I didn't have room to unpack after I came here from the manor," she explained, a little sadly. She gestured towards some others. "These belong to His Lordship, and these others belong to James. He said he would visit me, you know."

She led them further into the cellar which was proving to be quite extensive. The light from the one bulb didn't quite reach into these furthermost recesses and they had to pick their way carefully. Passing row after row of packing cases, they eventually turned a corner and reached a dead end.

"There now," she said.

It took a moment for their eyes to adjust but, after a few seconds, as they peered into the gloom they were able to just about make out the shape of an old wooden door set back in an alcove in the brick wall. Meg reached out, all but snatched the bunch of keys and pushed the large iron one into the keyhole. There was a satisfying click as the door was unlocked.

"Told you so," she crowed.

"Meg," began Charles, as calmly as he could, "it's really very kind of you to bring us down here but-"

"Oh, don't patronise me!" she snapped, in a rare moment of lucidity. "Do you want to get into my old room or not?"

"Well...yes. Yes, of course we do."

"Well then," and she pointed towards the door, "there's your way in."

Charles glanced with Matthew in the semi-gloom then reached forward and opened the door. It swung inwards noisily on hinges that desperately needed oiling.

"You'll be needing that," said Meg.

They turned and saw her pointing to a shelf a few feet away, on which lay a large battery-operated torch. Charles nodded and picked it up. Pointing it into the darkness he switched it on. The light from the torch revealed a short brick-walled passageway which opened up, after a few feet, into what appeared to be an extensive catacomb. They both gasped in amazement. Although Charles swung the beam of light left and right he was unable to gauge the extent of this vast underground cavern. Pillars supporting the vaulted ceiling stretched away from them in all directions.

Meg called after them, "you'll be alright as long as you walk in a straight line, it's not really very far...at least, I don't think it is...oh, I can't really remember. You need to be on the lookout for a staircase on the far side. Shall I put the kettle on for when you come back?"

The floor of the catacomb was damp and slippery. Water dripped from the ceiling and moss grew on many of the supporting columns. With only the light from the torch to guide them, Charles and Matthew edged forward cautiously, shivering each time another icy droplet fell and began to trickle down their necks.

"Do you really think we're going to find what we're looking for down here?" asked Matthew.

"To be honest, I'm not sure, but for a change Meg seemed pretty convinced that this was the way we needed to go. In any case, just at the moment I don't really have any alternative suggestions. Do you?" Matthew didn't reply. "And anyway," Charles continued, "You should look at this as an educational experience. How often do people ever get the chance to examine such a splendid piece of underground architecture?"

Matthew snorted and they continued their trudge further into the gloom.

Back in Heston Grange, meanwhile, James and Mrs Gillcarey were taking a well earned tea-break before resuming their duties.

"How do you think they're getting on?" asked Mrs Gillcarey.

James took a long gulp of tea. "They are making some progress," he said, "but Mr Seymour told me that at one point he thought he might have heard some rats behind a wall in the library."

Mrs Gillcarey looked at him over the top of her steaming mug and giggled.

After a while, Charles asked, "How far would you say it was when we walked from the house to the lodge?"

"I was just wondering the same thing. Surely we ought to be at least close by now."

"This place is vast! Why would anyone build an underground chamber like this?"

"Well, the sea is close by. Maybe it was used by smugglers in times past."

At length, the torchlight revealed that they were approaching another brick wall. Shining the light along its length they spotted an opening about thirty feet to the right. Their attempt at walking in a straight line through the darkness hadn't been too badly judged. The opening was, in fact, another short passageway, much like the one through which they had entered. After a few feet they found themselves standing at the bottom of a flight of spiral stone steps. Charles shone the torch into the gloom, but could only see the first few steps before the staircase curved away from view.

"I suppose these must be the steps Meg told us about."

"Unless there are other staircases out there in the dark?"

"Don't even think about it. Come on."

They had to tread carefully; the steps were eroded and uneven, so they were forced to ascend slowly. Not only that, but the staircase proved to be a high one. Eventually, their progress was blocked by what appeared to be a trapdoor above them.

"Could this be our journey's end?" wondered Charles aloud as he shone the light upwards.

"One way to find out," said Matthew. "Can you push it open?"

Charles handed the torch to down to Matthew and, with both hands now free, placed his palms against the flat surface above and pushed. Remarkably, it opened quite easily, swinging upwards and away from them on its hinges, reaching a resting position at just past ninety degrees. Without any further word being spoken both men quickly scrambled up and into the darkness beyond.

The illumination from the torch revealed a light switch on the wall and, a moment later, through blinking eyes they saw what they guessed must be the inside of the secret room. All those steps had

brought them up to the top floor, under the eaves, so the most immediately eye-catching feature of the room was its shape. The walls
sloped inwards, all meeting at a central point and looking rather like-

"It's like the inside of a pyramid!" exclaimed Charles. "What were
the words of that poem?

"In the still chamber of yon pyramid
Surely some Old-world Sphinx lurks deeply hid."

"We must be on the right track then," said Matthew. "Meg was
right about the key after all. Do you suppose there's a sphinx of some
sort hidden somewhere in here?"

"I presume so, and I guess we need to find it."

The room appeared to contain nothing, except for two items. The
first was a large wooden chest placed across one of the room's cor-
ners. They stood looking at it for a moment.

"Do you suppose a sphinx might be hiding in there?" asked
Charles.

Expecting it to be locked they were delighted to find that it was
not, but opening the lid revealed nothing; it was just an empty chest.

"Somehow, I knew it was never going to be that easy," Matthew
grumbled.

The second item was a small key which was hanging on a hook
by a door. The key fitted the lock and the door opened into the dark
corridor where the two of them had stood just a short time ago.

"So not an entirely wasted trip," said Charles, a little sarcastically,
"At least we've managed to find the key."

"The poem said that the sphinx was hidden deeply," said Matthew.
"Might that mean it's under the floor?"

They began to examine the bare floorboards to see if there was
any suggestion of some sort of concealed cavity beneath but, again,
their search proved fruitless.

Matthew's feelings of frustration were starting to rise again.

"Damn!" he shouted. "So what are we supposed to do now?"

Charles didn't respond. He was thinking. After a long moment
he spoke.

"I wonder how long ago Lord Alfred created this little treasure hunt?"

"What do you mean?"

"Well, if he made the film while this room was still occupied by Meg, then the sphinx in the poem could well have been something that was here in this room *at that time*. He wouldn't necessarily have spent time re-thinking all his carefully constructed clues just because a maid left his employment."

"Are you suggesting that we need to search through that mountain of packing cases in Meg's cellar?"

"We can hardly just go rifling through all her personal possessions. I mean, at least one of us wouldn't be comfortable with doing that; but I think we at least ought to go and have another talk with her."

Matthew sighed. "Oh, goody goody. I can hardly wait."

10

"But why?" Meg was asking. "Haven't you got better things to do than spend time looking for something like that? I've already told you it's worthless. It only holds sentimental value."

It wasn't that Charles was unwilling to explain the situation; he just knew that he wouldn't be understood. Once again sitting in Meg's small parlour, it occurred to Charles that trying to get the required information from Meg was rather like it had been in the old days trying to find out train information from a branch line ticket office.

"Meg," he tried again. "I am Lord Alfred's solicitor and in order that I can correctly settle his estate, according to his wishes, it is of the utmost importance that I find that missing sphinx. Can you tell us anything about it? Please."

"Why isn't James here? I thought you said he was going to visit me."

"As soon as I see him I will tell him."

"Thank you."

Another pause.

"Well...?"

"Well what?"

Matthew interrupted. "The sphinx, Meg! Where is it?"

"There's no need to shout. I'm not deaf, you know."

Motioning for Matthew to be silent, Charles spoke again, more softly. "Please, Meg. The sphinx?"

"Ah yes, the sphinx. Do you know where I got it? Many years ago, Lord and Lady Willoughby went for a holiday in the country and asked me to go along, to help look after them - not that I had any choice in the matter, naturally; a good servant knows their station in life, that's what James always says. Oh, I do wish he'd come. Anyway, one afternoon, Lady Willoughby wanted to take a nap, so Lord Willoughby and I went out walking by ourselves."

Meg paused, her gaze fixed on nothing in particular. Nothing, that is, except the memories in her mind at that moment.

"It just so happened that we came upon a country fair with all manner of stalls and sideshows. One of the stalls was selling something called 'do-it-yourself' sculptures. They weren't real sculptures, of course. You paid your money, selected a mould and filled it with plaster. Then they put it in some sort of oven and when you came back a little while later they peeled off the mould and there you were, feeling like Michaelangelo, with a little memento of your day to take home."

"So what happened?"

"Well, being in holiday mood, Lord Willoughby decided he'd like to have a go at this - he was quite an accomplished artist, you know? - and he asked me to choose a mould. There were lots to choose from, but in the end I chose the sphinx. When we collected the finished model later he gave it to me as a present."

"That's a lovely story, Meg."

"Where is it now?" asked Matthew.

"Where's what?"

"The sphinx!" Matthew was once again coming close to losing his temper.

"Oh, you do keep going on about it! Where's James?"

With a practised calmness in his voice, Charles asked, "Meg, is the sphinx in one of those packing cases in the cellar?"

"Of course it isn't. Why would I put it down there?"

"Did you leave it somewhere back at the manor?"

"No."

"Ok...well...did you put it in this room?"

"Yes."

Charles and Matthew were startled by this revelation and both looked round. There were ornaments aplenty throughout the room - on shelves, on the mantlepiece, on the window sill, even on top of the curtain pelmet...but none of them looked like a sphinx.

"Where, Meg? We can't see where you put it."

She gave a little smile and pointed to a low table in the corner, laden with knick-knacks and curios. In the centre was what looked like a jewelry box.

"I put it in there."

Matthew crossed the room in a single bound and picked up the box. Opening the lid he found that it was stuffed with many folds of thin black fabric, and it was clear from the indentations that something that was probably fragile had been kept inside, with the fabric used as cushioning. But whatever it had been was no longer there. Aside from the black material the box was empty.

"Oh dear," said Meg. "Is it not there after all?"

Matthew gave a cry of exasperation and dropped the box onto a chair.

"Temper, temper, young man," muttered Meg, then gave one of her little-old-lady chuckles. Turning to Charles, she said, "I do so wish James was here. I like you, you know."

"I like you too, Meg."

"Now, don't you patronise me, young man. I may be a servant but that doesn't mean I don't have a brain. You asked me if I put the sphinx in this room and I did." She smiled. "But later I moved it to somewhere else. I was about to tell you, but with the way you two have been shouting and carrying on I thought you needed to be taught a lesson."

There was a pause, while Meg regarded her two visitors with a stern stare as though they were naughty schoolboys.

"Well?" she asked.

"Well what?"

She rolled her eyes skyward. "Have you learnt your lesson?"

"Yes, Meg, we have and we're both very sorry - we're sorry, aren't we Matthew?"

"Oh...er...yeah. We're sorry." They both did their level best to appear suitably penitent.

"Hmm...well, just so long as you really *are*." She paused again, then seemed to reach a conclusion. "Very well then. The model you're looking for, which used to occupy that box, you'll now find on my bedside table in the other room, but please be careful with it."

Matthew was already on his way but Charles stopped him and indicated that he would fetch it, which he did in a manner which he hoped would appear a little less hasty. Returning to the room a few moments later he had a satisfied expression on his face as he carefully cradled the all-important and elusive sphinx. It was made of white plaster and, as he turned it over in his hands, a message came into view inscribed in the base:

To M. My tribute to Oscar's best. Love, A.

Meg was smiling wistfully again.

"When the stallholder passed the sphinx to Lord Alfred he warned him that the plaster would still be just a little soft. That was when His Lordship picked up a little piece of twig from the ground and wrote that message for me into the base. I felt so honoured; I mean...a personal message from Lord Alfred to me!"

"What did he mean by 'Oscar's best'?" asked Charles.

"I'm not sure. I did ask him, but he just smiled and said I would probably figure it out one day. I wondered whether perhaps it was something to do with the film award ceremony. Lord Alfred was well connected in those days and he so loved mixing with all those fine folk from the silver screen. What did you say your name was?"

"Charles. I'm Charles, and this is Matthew, Lord Alfred's son."

"Oh, I thought James was coming."

"Meg, we have to go now. Would it be alright if we borrowed the sphinx, just for a little while? We'll bring it back just as soon as our work is finished."

"Must you take it? I'm really very fond of it."

"We'll take great care of it, Meg. I promise."

"Very well, but please bring it back safely. I'm sure James would be happy to bring it back, if you asked him."

"Thank you. You have been very helpful," said Charles, as he placed the model carefully back into its fabric-lined box..

A moment later found Charles and Matthew standing on the short pathway leading to the gate in the white fence. The thunder had eased but the rain was heavier now, and it was decidedly chilly and almost dark.

"A good job we brought the car this time," said Matthew, holding the box containing the sphinx.

"True, but I think it may be about to run out of petrol."

"Very funny".

They walked as briskly as possible through the splattering raindrops towards the car. Charles climbed into the driving seat and slammed the door as quickly as he could, to avoid the rainwater landing on the plush interior; but Matthew didn't seem to care. After all, it wasn't his car. Charles started the engine and the heavy vehicle began to move back towards the house.

11

"I was beginning to wonder what had happened to you, sir," said James as he filled Charles' glass with a deep ruby Merlot from an exquisitely crafted decanter. As Charles received the glass, the flames from the hearth reflected and sparkled through the fruity liquid.

Outside, the darkness of night had closed in and, somewhere deep below stairs, Mrs Gillcarey was busily putting the finishing touches to yet another of her home-cooked gastronomic delights.

"That's kind of you, James. We went to pay Meg a visit at the Lodge."

"Yes, sir, Mrs Gillcarey mentioned that she had spoken to you about her, so I guessed that to be where you probably were. Have you been able to make any progress with the...er...puzzle?"

Matthew, sitting in a chair on the other side of the fireplace, spoke up.

"Yes and no. We did manage to locate this, which we think may be significant." He held up the sphinx and it was immediately clear that James recognised it.

"Dad mentioned a sphinx and a pyramid in his poem and we're confident that this is the sphinx he was referring to, but we're not quite sure how to progress from here."

"It has been a fair while since I last saw that model, sir," said James. "I believe it was a gift to Meg from His Lordship."

"Yes, that's correct, and she kindly agreed to lend it to us to help us solve the riddle," said Charles.

"She always was a kindly soul," said James, and then he added, a little sadly, "Was she...quite well when you saw her?"

"She was broadly coherent, but now and then her conversation would fly off at a tangent; and she kept saying she hoped you would visit her."

The elderly butler nodded.

"Yes, I do try to go and see her as often as my duties allow. I think that perhaps I should make a little more of an effort, but I find that her gradually worsening mental condition does distress me some-what. She was always such a joy in years gone by."

James turned away so as to keep Charles and Matthew from notic-ing as he dabbed a tear from the corner of his eye.

There was quiet then, and all three men were lost in their own thoughts, gazing into the flames which danced and crackled cheer-fully around the logs and red hot coals.

Eventually, Charles broke the silence.

"James, do you have any idea as to the possible significance of the name 'Oscar' in the inscription on the sphinx?"

He put his head back and thought for a moment.

"Not specifically, sir. I know that Lord Alfred was quite a follow-er of the Oscar film award ceremonies, mainly due to the circles in which he used to move in years gone by." Then he gave a little laugh. "There is also an oscar fish in the aquarium."

"Yes, I did notice that."

"I wonder if the inscription might be referring to that in some way?"

Just then a bell tinkled and James announced, "Ah, dinner is served, gentlemen."

They moved over to the large table and waited for what they knew would be a treat. Not for the first time, Charles was thinking that he was being rather spoiled at Heston Grange.

This time, the meal was cod and haddock dauphinoise, and it was cooked to perfection. Mrs Gillcarey positively rippled with pleasure when Charles and Matthew complimented her on both its taste and texture.

"I'm not convinced that the connection between the sphinx and the Oscar awards is the right one," said Charles, between mouthfuls. "I think that's a red herring."

"No pun intended?" asked Matthew, indicating the delicious chunks of juicy fish on his plate. As they continued to feast he quipped, "If that oscar fish does have something to do with our little mystery, I hope he hasn't made an appearance in this fish dinner!"

Charles laughed - then froze. Matthew saw the sudden change.

"What's wrong?" he asked.

"I do believe I've got it," said Charles.

"Got what?"

"This reference to 'Oscar'. I bet it has nothing to do with films or fish."

"What is it then?"

"Isn't it obvious? Lord Alfred loved poetry. Surely he's talking about Oscar Wilde!"

"I thought Wilde only wrote stories."

"That's what he's most famous for, but he wrote a good number of poems too."

"But we've been through every book of poetry in the library... haven't we?"

They both realised simultaneously that they had, in fact, not done so.

"We were working our way through alphabetically," recalled Charles, "but we stopped when we found the book of handwritten poems."

"I was looking through a book of Tennyson at that moment," said Matthew.

"I can't quite remember what I was looking at," said Charles, "but I'm sure we hadn't reached 'W' yet."

Risking the onset of indigestion, they gobbled the rest of their dinner, giving their apologies to Mrs Gillcarey who, having re-entered the room bearing a delightfully tempting tiramisu, was more than a little disappointed as they left her standing there and hurried back to the library, where they began to scan the shelves once again.

Sure enough, there were several small books devoted to the poet, but one in particular caught Charles' eye. It was larger than the others and stood at the end of the shelf, almost acting as a book-end.

"I bet that's the one," he said, pointing to the title on its spine. It read, *"The Best of Oscar Wilde."*

"My tribute to Oscar's best," breathed Matthew. "Yes, that must be it."

Carefully, he slid the book from the shelf and set it down on the reading desk.

"It feels quite light for such a large book," he observed.

He moved to open the cover but found that he could not do so. It was then that they realised that this was not a book at all. In fact, it was a cleverly disguised box - which was locked.

"Let's just break the ruddy thing open," said Matthew.

In a flash of inspiration, Charles asked, "Do you still have the bunch of keys from Meg?"

"Yes, I do...here."

Charles tried one after another, with increasing frustration, but then he drew a sharp intake of breath as one of the keys finally turned and the lock clicked open. Slowly and carefully, he lifted the lid. What was visible at first were the now familiar folds of thin black fabric, which appeared to fill the box. With trembling fingers, Charles began to carefully move the folds of material aside. He gasped as the light reflected on something blue - the sapphire? But then, as he continued to unfold the cypress cloth, they both suddenly saw what it actually was, and a tingle of excitement ran through them both.

Looking up at them from the box, snugly and smugly enrobed among the folds of black fabric, was a blue plastic spool - a second roll of cine film.

12

As the camera started to whirr and hum once again, both Matthew and Charles felt like small children on Christmas Day. They had viewed the first film on a bright sunny morning - had it really only been a couple of days ago? Now they were seeing the second instalment late at night with another violent storm raging outside.

His Lordship had, again, selected the octagonal tower room as the location from which to deliver his oration. At first, all that was to be seen was the reading desk, but then Lord Alfred himself made his entrance, in a very similar manner to that adopted for the previous occasion. Immaculately attired in his velvet smoking jacket he walked round to his leather upholstered chair behind the desk and sat. He regarded his amateur detectives from the screen for a long moment before drawing breath to speak.

"Well, well, well," he began, "I suppose I should start by saying that I'm impressed - although, of course, I don't know for certain who I'm speaking to. I'm fairly sure that at least Charles will be seeing this film - I doubt Matthew would have been able to follow the trail on his own."

Matthew squirmed in his seat.

"So, if he is there, the two of you must have teamed up. That would be a rather mature thing to do, wouldn't it? Well, maybe there's hope for you after all." He paused for a moment, then gave a wry smile and continued.

"Anyway, it would seem that you managed to solve my little sphinx puzzle. Well done. Did you know, according to mythology, the sphinx was a creature that would set riddles for unwary travellers and then strangle them if they couldn't give the correct answer? Somehow that seems to be rather apt, wouldn't you say? And what did you think of my cryptic lines? Even though I do say so myself, I found them to be quite ingenious in the circumstances."

He paused again, seeming to consider his next words carefully.

"And, if you'll listen to my advice, there are still one or two more clues to be unearthed within them."

He gave a little chuckle that might have been a sneer.

"Shall I tell you a secret? For once in my miserable life I'm actually starting to enjoy myself. I hope you're having as much fun as I am."

"You don't know the half of it," grumbled Matthew.

"Now then," Lord Alfred cleared his throat. "I have another little clue which I'm sure will interest you. Pay attention, class; here it comes."

And, with that, he began to recite a second piece of verse:

> *"Ah! sweet indeed to rest within the womb*
> *Of Earth. Great mother of eternal sleep,*
> *But sweeter far for thee a restless tomb*
> *In the blue cavern of an echoing deep,*
> *Or where the tall ships founder in the gloom*
> *Against the rocks of some wave-shattered steep."*

If the reading of the first poem had been in the style of Gielgud, this second performance was definitely an Olivier. There could be no denying that he did bring a true quality to his delivery. Appearing to read the minds of his audience, he sighed and said, "Did you like that? Maybe I should have been a thespian. Incidentally," he added, "in creating this little treasure hunt for you, I thought it might be rather nice to take the opportunity to indulge not only my great love of poetry but also my love of painting too. I hope that meets with your approval?" He raised an eyebrow as if expecting to hear a response.

"Well, I think that should give you what you need for the next stage and it brings us all up to date once more. Do enjoy the game - joy in the journey, that's what it's all about."

He stood up and made as if to leave, but then suddenly looked back into the camera and said, "But don't forget, time is of the essence. I am sure my friends down at the Society of West End Theatre would be only too happy if you did not manage to solve this quaint conundrum sufficiently quickly."

He cackled, mischievously.

"Well, I must be going now. As one of my old teachers used to say, 'Onwards and downwards.' Farewell."

He walked away from the desk and, as before, disappeared from the left side of the screen. A moment later the film ended, and both men sat quietly in the dark, trying to absorb the significance of what they had just heard.

"The fact that both films start and end with His Lordship out of range of the camera would suggest that he was alone when he did the filming," said Charles. "He probably started and stopped the camera himself."

"So what if he did?" asked Matthew.

"Nothing. Just an observation."

Matthew looked over to the imposing grandfather clock which stood against the wall as though it were on sentry duty. It was almost midnight.

"Well," he said, "I'm too exhausted to give this any thought now; let's get some sleep."

"Good idea," Charles replied. "Then hopefully we'll be able to make a fresh start with this new clue in the morning."

With the storm so far showing no sign of abating, the two men walked out of the library and headed for their respective rooms.

13

Charles closed his bedroom door and leaned his head back against it. He realised that in the last few days he had used up a huge amount of nervous mental energy, not to mention the physical exertion of walking for miles all over the house and creeping around in those underground catacombs, and it was starting to catch up with him. He was no longer quite the spring chicken he used to be and the sudden feeling of fatigue that descended upon him caused him almost to go straight to sleep on the bed just as he was, fully clothed.

Somehow, though, he managed to get himself ready for bed properly. A minute later, as he slid between the crisp, clean sheets he knew he had made the right choice. Just one minute more and he was fast asleep and dreaming. But it was a restless slumber at first: all kinds of pictures flew through his mind...the stark shape of Heston Grange illumined by sudden flashes of lightning...dark corridors and secret passageways...delicious dinners in front of roaring fires...and the faces...faces blurring and merging and re-emerging as other faces...Lord Alfred...James...Matthew...Mrs Gillcarey...Meg...and even his ex-fiance put in an appearance, suddenly transforming into a sphinx, laughing hysterically on a swaying rickety bridge. Gradually, the images faded and, as he tossed and turned beneath his luxurious blankets, Charles moved, little by little, into a deeper and sounder sleep.

Some distance away, Matthew stood in his room also contemplating his bed. Despite his tiredness, though, he was deep in thought. He recalled the terms of this ludicrous contest as set out by his father in the first film:

"There's nothing in this game for coming second. The winner takes all."

What was his father thinking of? Who was this Charles anyway? Only a two-bit solicitor like all the rest. Why should Charles have any claim on the vast fortune that should rightfully pass to him? He sighed and thought about the agreement he had made with Charles. True, it was only a verbal one but it was still an agreement, and Charles was obviously a decent fellow, in his own way. If they continued to work together and managed to solve the riddle they would divide the estate equally. That was what they had agreed - but what if Matthew somehow managed to crack this puzzle alone, and what if he managed to find the sapphire without any further involvement on Charles' part? He felt sure that most of the deduction process was now behind them. The situation, as it stood right now, was that there was this new clue on the cine film...and Charles was sleeping. After thinking for just a moment longer, Matthew reached a decision. Quietly, he eased open his bedroom door, crept out stealthily onto the landing and, while attempting to avoid stepping on any squeaky floorboards, once again entered the labyrinthine network of dark corridors.

He came, at length, into the dining room where the dying embers of the fire were still exuding a dull red glow. Crossing to the fireplace he looked at the high-backed chair where he had been sitting before dinner. The sphinx was still there, just where he had left it. He picked it up and turned it over in his hands, once again reading the inscription underneath. Did this model still have any light to shed on the mystery, he wondered. Certainly, in the second film his father had mentioned that the first set of cryptic lines still contained some further clues. He moved over to the large bay window and looked in the direction of the private cemetery, hidden from view by the many wind-blown trees. Something inside told him, despite his earlier search, that there must be some sort of clue to be found out there.

Both poems were infused with references to such a place. Surely the sapphire had to be there. Where else could it be? But something else inside also told him that if he was going to explore the cemetery again he would have to do it tonight. Now - while Charles slept on, blissfully unaware. He gazed out into the deeply black night. The rain was fierce, and the strong wind repeatedly lashed the window panes. The creaking of boughs and branches as they swayed back and forth through huge arcs could be clearly heard through the howling gale. Did he really want to venture out...out into that? Would he be able to find anything anyway, in the darkness? And, if he did, could he be absolutely sure that he would not be spotted?

"Can I help you, sir?"

The deep voice spoke right next to him. With a cry of surprise, Matthew spun round and, as he did so, the sphinx slipped from his grip. As it slid away he tried to grasp it again but it fell and hit the wooden floor with a loud crack, shattering into several pieces with tiny shards of white plaster flying in all directions.

"Oh, I am sorry, sir. It was not my intention to startle you."

"That's ok, James. Er...I couldn't sleep. Here, let me help you clean up the mess."

"Please don't trouble yourself, sir. I can manage. Would you like me to bring you a cup of warm milk? They say that it's really most helpful if you're having difficulty sleeping."

"Thanks, but you don't need to worry. I'm sure I'll drop off eventually." He tried to inject a jaunty tone into his voice, though without much success. "Well, goodnight."

"Goodnight, sir."

With a furrowed brow, James watched as Matthew left the room and disappeared into the darkness. Then he turned and, with the storm beyond the window still at full force, began to collect up the broken pieces of the sphinx.

14

Although the rain had stopped it was still very windy and the sky was grey and overcast as Charles and Matthew breakfasted together the following morning.

Charles wasn't sure, but thought he detected a slight tension in the air whenever James and Matthew exchanged any conversation. He did not really give it much thought, however - his mind was far too occupied with trying to discover the significance of the new poem.

"Well," he began, "I was hoping that sleeping on the problem would yield some answers, or at least some sort of idea as to how we might proceed, but I'm afraid I've come up blank; and we now have one day less in which to reach the end of this riddle." He paused as he chewed a mouthful of seeded granary toast topped with a generous spoonful of well-textured homemade gooseberry preserve. "Have you had any new thoughts, Matthew?"

He nodded as James offered to refill his cup and watched as the rich, steaming beverage bubbled forth from the silver coffee pot.

"Erm...no, not really." Matthew seemed slightly distant this morning, thought Charles.

"Is everything alright?" he asked.

With the briefest of glances in James' direction, Matthew leaned forward and said, "Actually, I have a confession to make."

"Oh?" Charles raised an eyebrow.

"Well...er...did you sleep ok last night? Did anything disturb you?"

"I slept like a log. Didn't you?"

"Yes...no. Well...I couldn't sleep at first, so I went down into the dining room to find the sphinx. I thought that looking at it again might give me some inspiration or something. Since I was still wide awake I thought I might as well try and do something useful."

"Ok, and..?"

"Well, I managed to break it, didn't I? I dropped it on the wooden floor. It would probably have been alright if it had fallen on the carpet, but I had to be standing on the bare floorboards by the window just at that moment."

"Meg especially asked us to take care of it."

"I know that!" he snapped. Then, more quietly, "Sorry."

"If I may, gentlemen?"

"Yes, James?"

"When I collected the broken pieces, instead of throwing them away I took the liberty of taking them back to my room where I laid them out and, with a little care and patience, I think I could make a reasonably good attempt at repairing the model, if you'd like me to try."

"I suppose it would be better than nothing," said Charles, "but it'll still be rather embarassing when we give it back to Meg."

"There's always the chance she might just have forgotten all about it?" suggested Matthew.

"Well, you never know how some people are going to react in certain circumstances do you, sir?"

The ever-so-slightly pointed tone of the butler's remark was not lost on Matthew who shot a dark knowing look at James; but Charles didn't seem to notice.

"Well, we shall just have to hope," he said, "that our little sphinx was not concealing any further clues. If it was, we might now be really sunk."

Matthew decided to change the subject. "I did have a thought about those two poems, though."

"Yes?"

"Well, since they both focus on the theme of death or, more specifically, graves, maybe we should go and take another look at the cemetery in the grounds. I did explore it once already but that was before we had unravelled some of the clues. Perhaps now, with two of us, we might spot something important."

James interjected again, "Forgive me gentlemen but, if I may say so, I find it most encouraging that you have opted to work together to solve this mystery. The spirit of co-operation between you is really very heart-warming."

Matthew glanced at him. "Thank you, James. Do you have any duties to attend to?"

"Yes, sir. Very good, sir." He turned and left.

"That was a little harsh, wasn't it?" asked Charles.

Matthew shrugged. "Yeah, right. Shall we go and look at some graves?"

With coats firmly fastened and collars turned up to protect themselves from the biting wind they set out towards the cemetery. As they neared their destination, Charles became aware that although they were walking in the direction of the sea the sound of the waves appeared to actually diminish as they neared the white fence with its small gate. The phenomenon became even more remarkable as they entered the graveyard itself; once inside, the noise vanished altogether.

"How extraordinary," he commented, "that these tall hedges and trees manage to block out the sound so completely."

Matthew just gave another of his trademark shrugs.

"When I was here the first time," he said, "I thought that perhaps the poem was referring to that large grave at the far end. It has cypress trees, and the flat white slab on top could be described as a sun-bleached stone. I didn't find anything useful though." Inwardly, he was still smarting at the caustic note that he had found waiting for him, but he wasn't going to mention that to Charles.

"Actually," said Charles, "virtually all the trees in here seem to be cypresses. Anyway, let's look round and see if we can find anything helpful."

They separated and began picking their way over the once well-kept but now overgrown and uneven terrain. They peered at tombstones and tried to make out the inscriptions. They looked at the cypress trees and wondered whether it was to a particular one or two that the poem was referring. They trudged back and forth, looking for something - anything - that might give some sort of pointer. At length, all they found was cold and disappointment.

"There's nothing here," said Charles, eventually. "Even if there was something, we're not going to find it by just traipsing about randomly. We need something more precise and specific to go on."

"And it's cold," added Matthew, stating the obvious. "Let's go get some tea."

Back in the library, with their circulation gradually returning, they nibbled on some of Mrs Gillcarey's oaty flapjacks and drank from large mugs of lapsang souchong tea, the rich flavour bringing a re-assuring, comforting feeling, albeit an illusory one, to the situation.

"Perhaps we should watch both films again," said Matthew.

"Why not?"

"Next, we'll be opening our very own cinema."

"Very witty."

As the second roll of film came to an end yet again Charles and Matthew remained staring at the vacant screen as, for the umpteenth time, they combed through Lord Alfred's words in their minds.

"I agree that both poems could well be alluding to that cemetery," said Charles. "Their theme is quite obviously centred around graves and death."

"Yes, and what did he mean when he said he wanted to indulge his love of painting?" asked Matthew.

Charles sighed. "I don't have the faintest idea. At least, not yet." There was another pause, then he took a deep breath.

"Let's assess what we have so far. We have the first poem, the so-called cryptic lines, which we then find are written in Lord Alfred's hand, in duplicate and back to back in such a way that a floor plan of the house is created. That leads us to the location of a secret room -"

"-which we can't get into until we've talked our way past an old crone whose brain has atrophied," interrupted Matthew.

"Once we do get inside we find that it that looks like a pyramid, and we deduce that it once contained a sphinx. After further talking with Meg we manage to find the sphinx -"

"- which is now broken."

"And that leads us to the disguised box containing the second film. That is where we hear another poem and we're told, rather intriguingly, that the first one still contains clues. We also learn that His Lordship wants to bring his painting skills into the mix." He paused. "Have I missed anything?"

"Just one small detail."

"Oh?"

Matthew stood up and began to pace back and forth, angrily.

"The clock is ticking and time is running out. Let's suppose that we do manage to make some headway with this second poem. What then? Are we to discover yet another film hidden under the floorboards? And then another one stuffed inside a reindeer head in the trophy room? And then do we find we have to recite the complete works of Shakespeare backwards, in Swahili? Or does this wild goose chase even have an end at all? I wouldn't be surprised if the old codger deliberately set out to make the task so long and complicated that we couldn't possibly solve it in the time allowed."

Charles took another swig of tea, discovering too late that it was now unpleasantly tepid. Then a thought struck him.

"I wonder..." he began.

Matthew momentarily paused in his pacing and glanced over at him.

"I wonder whether Lord Alfred was being more crafty than we've quite realised."

"What do you mean?"

"Well, the artistic lettering of the first poem provided us with a plan of the house, but additionally the actual content of the text mentioned the pyramid room and also told us about the sphinx."

"Yes...so?"

"I'm thinking that maybe each clue has more than one meaning."

"Oh, well that's just great. So at a stroke we've doubled the size of the task."

"Wait. Can we identify which clues have so far appeared to lead in only one direction?"

It didn't take them long to work it out.

"The sphinx!" said Matthew. "The inscription in the base led us to the box with the second roll of film, but up to now that's all. Could it be trying to tell us something else in addition?"

Charles was thinking. "Hmm...maybe."

"But it's broken," Matthew lamented.

"I suppose we could ask James to bring us the broken pieces - that might yield something."

"Perhaps there was something hidden inside it?"

"I would've thought that was unlikely. If Lord Alfred did put something inside it he would need to have done so when the model was first made before the plaster had set. Surely he couldn't have planned this little escapade so long ago?"

"Wouldn't put it past him."

"Just a minute...what did the inscription say? *My tribute to Oscar's best.*"

"Yes, from which we found the box."

"It was cleverly disguised to look like a book – a book of what?"

"Stories or poems, I assume. It was called 'The best of Oscar Wilde.'"

"But inside, there weren't any poems - only the film."

Matthew was becoming restless again.

"Ok, so what of it?"

"This entire quest has been hallmarked with poetry from start to finish - but we haven't yet looked at any of Oscar Wilde's actual poems!"

Matthew hesitated before saying, thoughtfully, "Yes, you're right."

They moved quickly along the library shelves yet again and found the small number of Oscar Wilde volumes. Charles handed three of them to Matthew and took the other three himself.

"Once again, I don't know what we're looking for," he said, "but let's hope we recognise it when we see it."

They settled themselves into the two comfy chairs and began to read.

It was barely three minutes later when Matthew suddenly exclaimed, "I've got it!"

Charles leapt up and crossed over to him.

"What have you found?"

"See for yourself."

Matthew handed him the book, holding it open at a certain page, then sat back in his chair folding his arms in satisfaction. Charles took one look and gave a wry smile. "So the poems were not Lord Alfred's own creations after all."

The two poems, with which Charles and Matthew were now both very familiar, were in fact two halves of the same poem. Written by Oscar Wilde, it was entitled "The Grave of Shelley."

15

"He could have told us the title right at the start when he made the first film, but he didn't."

Charles was pacing up and down and thinking aloud as he sought to assimilate what this new discovery could mean.

"He could also have included it with the two handwritten versions in his book, but he didn't do that either. Clearly, he made a conscious decision to deliberately keep the title a secret until this point."

"He made the assumption that neither of us would possess a sufficient knowledge of poetry to immediately recognise the poem in the first place."

"A safe assumption, as it turns out. Anyway, now that we know that it's just a single poem, and written about Shelley's final resting place, where does that take us?"

"I don't know. Did Shelley write poems too?"

Charles thought for a moment. "Hmm...not sure. If he did, I'm sure they'll be here on these shelves."

"Let's look."

"We're going to be quite well read by the time we're done."

Matthew smiled. "Here's a thought. Do you think this Shelley was any relation to Mary Shelley, who wrote 'Frankenstein'? Dad was always a bit of a monster."

Charles smiled back.

"Just find his poems and then find some clues."

They searched, and read, then read some more, and searched again, but it was heavy going. Prior to this whole incident Matthew had never so much as even picked up a book of poetry but now here he was, wading through numerous poems by this bloke, Shelley, and being faced with titles such as 'Song of Proserpine' and 'Adonais.' When he turned the page and came across a piece of writing entitled 'Ozymandias' he all but threw the book on the floor in despair. Time was passing and, despite the burst of euphoria when the title of the Wilde poem was discovered, further progress was now proving elusive. The ticking of the stately grandfather clock was the only sound as the two men read, serving as a constant reminder to them both that the deadline was drawing inexorably closer.

That evening, after hours of reading with nothing to show for their efforts, Charles and Matthew sat hunched over their dinners feeling miserable. Even the best efforts of the inestimable Mrs Gillcarey with her expertly prepared roast pork did little to lift their spirits, despite the tastiness of the crackling; but James did his job well and was constantly on hand to refill their glasses with mulled wine and, after the meal as they sat once again before the open fire, he left them with a handsome cheeseboard and a full decanter of vintage port.

They sipped - Matthew rather more than Charles - and gazed deeply into the cheerful flames, each lost in their thoughts.

"What are we not seeing?" mused Charles. "It can't be that difficult to spot. What the blazes is it?"

"Maybe we should be focussing on the comment about the painting?" suggested Matthew. "That one has drawn a complete blank so far."

"Yes, perhaps you're right." Charles paused for a moment, then continued. "Ok, how about this? Given that we now know that Lord Alfred copied out, by hand, poems which were not his own in order to provide us with the necessary clues, might he have done a similar sort of thing with his paintings?"

"You mean he might have painted copies of original pictures? Who knows? I suppose it's possible; but, if so, where are these mysterious 'illegal' counterfeits?"

"I suppose the idea is a bit far fetched. It would've involved a huge amount of work."

Just then, James came back into the room.

"Will there be anything else this evening, gentlemen?"

"No thank you, James." Then he added, "Oh, on second thoughts, actually, yes there is!"

The butler turned back to face them. "Yes, sir?"

"Given all these secret doorways and disguised keyholes we've been finding, do you happen to know whether there might be some secret hideaway in the house where Lord Alfred kept any of his paintings safely stashed away?"

"Not exactly, sir."

"What do you mean?"

"His Lordship's interest in painting was mainly centred on the collecting of fine works, rather than the creating of them. While you have been walking through the house you will no doubt have seen some of them."

Matthew looked downwards, suddenly feeling less than intellectual. He may indeed have walked past some valuable paintings, but he knew he wouldn't have recognised them for what they were. He knew what the Mona Lisa looked like but that was about it - and even he knew that *that* was one painting which his dad would not have been able to obtain.

"But," continued James, "on those rare occasions when he was a little less busy it was true that he would sometimes try his hand at producing something himself."

"Do you know where any of these paintings are?"

"Oh yes, sir, but they are not 'stashed away' as you put it. Having gone to the trouble of painting a picture he wanted it to be on display, but -" he paused.

"Please go on."

"Well," and here James gave a gentle laugh, "His Lordship instructed me to hang his paintings only in the darker corridors of the house. I think he was being just a little over-modest, since it is very seldom that we have any visitors; and, in any case, many of his pictures are really quite commendable. I think he felt that perhaps his efforts should not really be compared to those of the great masters."

"I see. Well, if I've learnt one thing since being at Heston Grange, it's that this house is enormous. We'll need your help, James. Could you take us round and show us which pictures were painted by Lord Alfred?"

"Erm...do you mean right now, sir? Is it perhaps just a little on the late side?"

Indeed it was. Charles glanced at the clock and discovered it was already past midnight.

"Good grief!" he exclaimed. "Where does all the time go?"

"*Tempus fugit*, sir." said James.

"Ok, well perhaps we could have an early breakfast and then be given the grand tour straight after that?"

"Very good, sir."

James gave a respectful inclination of the head, and left.

Charles, drained his glass and stood up, yawning. "I think I'll turn in too. A busy day ahead. See you in the morning."

"Yeah. I'll be going to bed too, as soon as I finish my port. Sleep well."

Matthew was left alone and re-filled his glass. Deep in thought, he stared into the diminishing fire for quite some time.

16

The next morning, Mrs Gillcarey was only a little disgruntled that her two guests refused her offer of second helpings of herb-infused bubble and squeak with hash browns. She clucked with disappointment but to no avail; the two of them were obviously keen to get on and discover whatever they could about Lord Alfred's personal contribution to the art world.

The three-man expedition set forth. Even though the weather to-day was mild, as they began to enter those regions of the mansion which were explored less frequently, it was reinforced once again to both Charles and Matthew that this was indeed a very old house. The wind could be heard whistling and whining through all manner of nooks and crannies. As they passed certain arched openings, they would feel a cold draught; elsewhere, a lattice window in a decaying frame would suddenly rattle. And everywhere there was the dust, causing Charles to vividly recall the first night of his visit when Lord Alfred had so dramatically destroyed his Will.

At length, after taking numerous turnings along endless passage-ways, James stopped by a moderately sized canvas in a simple wooden frame. He shone his torch upon it.

"This is one of His Lordship's paintings," he said.

Charles and Matthew leaned forward, trying to get a good view of it despite the surrounding gloom. There did not appear to be anything particularly special about the picture; as the light from the torch moved slowly back and forth it was revealed to be a simple landscape with rolling hills and a few grazing sheep, some nicely depicted cumulonimbus - and a couple of trees in the foreground which they both now knew to be cypress trees.

"Do you suppose that's in any way significant?" asked Matthew.

"Difficult to say, but it looks as though this picture was painted quite some time ago. Is it likely that it has any direct relevance?"

"Maybe, maybe not, but these cypress trees are making a habit of constantly turning up."

"True. Well, let's keep that in mind for possible future reference. Where's the next one, James?"

"This way, gentlemen."

They set off again, with Charles feeling very glad that they had James guiding them through the intricate network of otherwise unfathomable thoroughfares.

Some time later, James paused by another picture. "This one," he explained, "is of the view out to sea from the promontory not far from here. During a spell of fine weather His Lordship walked each day to a vantage point on top of the cliffs and, as I recall, took a great deal of care with painting the crest of each wave. In the end, he seemed to be rather pleased with the results of his efforts."

This was indeed a fine piece of work. The sunlight glinted off the water and the detail gradually faded most convincingly as the eye scanned upward towards the vanishing point on the horizon.

"But are there any clues here?" prompted Matthew.

"None that I can see," said Charles.

And so the day wore on. They saw painting after painting several of which, it had to be said, were really quite well done; others, perhaps less so - maybe these came from Lord Alfred's early period, Charles joked. But whether any of them served to advance their cause was anyone's guess. This artistic tour was, as it turned out, so long that the intrepid explorers missed out on lunch altogether and mid-afternoon found them back in their usual haunt - the library - this time with cups of Darjeeling and some delightfully gooey chocolate brownies.

"If we ever do manage to solve this mystery," said Charles, licking the delicious crumbs from his fingertips before reaching for his third slice, "the first thing I shall do is increase Mrs Gillcarey's wages!"

"That might not be such a good idea," Matthew replied. "I can feel those calories settling aready!"

The screen and projector were still set up in the same positions they had been occupying for the last several days. The two men ate and drank, lapsing into silence, as they both sat staring at the empty screen wondering whether they needed to watch the two films yet again and, if so, whether they could stand to do so. Matthew, especially, was sure that he could now recite the entire contents of each by heart.

The screen was standing against the one wall of the library which was not lined from floor to ceiling with books. Charles found himself looking beyond the screen to this wall, covered with traditional oak panelling and all those portraits in their oval shaped frames. On impulse, he rose from his chair, crossed the room and began to walk along this gallery of the great and the good. Something was trying to surface from his subconscious mind. After years as a practising solicitor he had grown to recognise the feeling. But what was it? Some detail in one of these portraits? Or was it perhaps something from one of the landscapes they had seen earlier? Maybe his brain was at last starting to piece together some hitherto unrecognised clues from Lord Alfred's films. He frowned, aware that some subliminal thought process was taking place but unable to formulate it fully, just at the moment. He walked along the rows of portraits again, on full mental alert. Here was a picture of Shakespeare. There was one of Robert Burns, and another showing William Wordsworth...and then he saw it.

"Matthew," he said, quietly. "Come and look at this."

"What is it?"

"Have a look at all these portraits. Do you see anything unusual?"

Matthew looked. "Nothing springs to mind."

"Which one would you say is the odd one out?"

"They're all pretty much the same. Oh, hang on a moment; I suppose that one's slightly different. It has a background."

And that was the crucial detail.

With this one exception, all the portraits had a dark coloured nondescript brown-grey background; but this one was different.

"The one with the scenic background," explained Charles, is a portrait of our friend, Shelley."

He looked up, sharply. "Ok, you have my attention."

"Look at it, Matthew. Don't you see what I see?"

He looked back at the face of Shelley staring impassively from the frame, and moved closer.

Then he gasped, speaking softly. "This is an old portrait," he whispered, "but I do believe that the background was added only recently."

"I think so too, but why?"

"How am I supposed to know?"

"For crying out loud, Matthew, look at it! Doesn't it strike you as being rather familiar?"

He looked again...and his mouth fell open as realisation dawned.

Lord Alfred had given them a poem entitled 'Shelley's Grave.' Here was a portrait of Shelley with a recently added background. This new background showed, of all things, a cemetery; one which they both knew about - the very one which was only a short distance away from where they now stood.

"He added a picture of Heston Grange cemetery into the background of the portrait," said Matthew, suddenly full of excitement.

"Yes, but look again. What else can you see?"

As Matthew pondered, Charles could no longer contain himself; he reached out an excited finger and pointed.

Among the various graves now familiar to them both, this newly added detail also showed a large flat white slab embedded into the ground. It was overshadowed with cypress trees.

"The sun bleached stone?" asked Matthew.

"I'd put money on it. We didn't see it before because it's hidden under all those creepers and brambles!"

"Do you fancy exploring some tombs?"

"I thought you'd never ask. Let's go!"

17

This time Charles and Matthew all but sprinted to the cemetery, roughly throwing open the gate and rushing inside in a manner which was quite the opposite of that adopted by most visitors to such places. Walking slowly back and forth, they carefully picked their way over the tangle of vines and branches. Taking the relative positions of the various graves into account, they eventually made an estimation as to where the crucial sun-bleached stone was likely to be concealed. The corner of the cemetery housed an old wooden shed, virtually hidden from view behind a straggling privet hedge. This shed was found to contain a selection of gardening implements which had certainly seen better days. Charles and Matthew returned, each armed with a rusty rake, with which they began to pull at the overgrown vegetation. Dozens of insects went scurrying away as their homes were ransacked, and clouds of spores and seed heads became airborne, lodging in their hair and clothing, but they paid no attention. It was but the work of a few seconds before a white stone began to appear beneath the numerous layers of old leaves and twigs. There was no need to speak. They moved and acted as one man, and soon the entire white rectangle was uncovered. They paused and stood, gardening tools still in hand, gazing down at it.

A plain, white slab.

Nothing else.

No cryptic poem this time.

"I was expecting it to have had some sort of inscription," said Charles.

"I don't want to be the one to spoil the party," said Matthew, "but do we know for certain that this is the stone we're looking for? There could be others hidden beneath all this rubbish."

They turned and surveyed the graveyard and it was immediately apparent that to clear the whole site would be a mammoth task.

"But we both saw the painting. This must be the right place. Look where the cypress trees are."

Matthew had to agree that this did seem to be the correct location.

Charles spoke again. "Alright, let's assume for a moment that we have uncovered the same stone that we saw in the portrait. It would appear, however, that there is no message waiting for us here. So what should we be looking for instead?"

"I hope we're not expected to go hunting for something underneath it. It must weigh a ton!"

Suddenly, Charles dropped his rake. His arms hung loosely at his sides and he stared straight ahead into mid-air.

"Are you ok?" asked Matthew.

"Could it really be that simple?" Charles murmured.

"What do you mean?"

"However unwittingly, you may well have hit the proverbial nail squarely on the head."

"In what way?"

"If there *is* something underneath this slab, given that we are standing in a cemetery, what might it be?"

"Well, I would hope it would be that wretched sapphire!"

Charles shook his head. "Not quite yet, I think. Matthew, what are cemeteries for?"

"Oh, I have no idea. Might they sometimes be used for burying dead people?"

"Are dead people ever put anywhere else?"

"Yes, there's the crematorium although I don't see many of those nearby. Sometimes they'll be entombed in a mausoleum, or perhaps a crypt."

Charles smiled.

"In both films, Lord Alfred has been constantly referring to the cryptic lines," he said. "I wonder if what he meant was literally 'crypt-ic'?"

"Are you suggesting that there might be an actual crypt underneath this stone?"

Charles picked up his rake, held it with its metal comb uppermost, and brought the wooden handle down onto the stone with a sharp crack. The dull thud which they would have expected did not occur. What they actually heard was a resonant, hollow sound.

"You have any better ideas?"

"Now that you mention it, no I don't."

Matthew ran back to the old wooden shed and returned with a couple of shovels and pickaxes. Charles examined the edge of the stone carefully, looking for any indication that would suggest how they should try to lift it.

"I think it'll just have to be trial and error," he said.

They each pushed the sharp edge of a pickaxe into the turf immediately adjoining the edge of the stone, working it downwards, then pulling back on the handle to try and gain purchase underneath the slab itself. As they applied leverage, the stone began to give, and they heard the earthy sound of soil and turf starting to separate.

"It's working!" shouted Matthew. The slab was lifting, albeit reluctantly.

They heaved and strained, through gritted teeth. It wasn't just a little heavy; it was seriously weighty. As the angle of the stone increased, beads of sweat fell from their foreheads. Charles thought he was going to faint.

"Keep going!" Matthew yelled.

Charles shut his eyes and summoned all his strength.

"We'll do a big pull on three!"

With the sinews in his neck clearly outlined, Charles managed the smallest of nods to show that he understood.

"One!....Two!....THREEEEE!!"

They both let out a roar, and pulled on their pickaxe handles with every ounce of effort they could muster. The stone slab reached the vertical, teetered for a moment, then fell over completely, landing on a mound of tangled branches. There was the sound of dry wood snapping as the stone came to rest, but neither Charles nor Matthew noticed. They stood transfixed, their attention held by the narrow flight of stone steps descending into the ground. Scarcely able to contain himself, Charles spoke a line from the poem, *'Here doth the little night owl make her home'*. At the same moment, he pointed down at the first step. There, clearly engraved in the surface, was the carving of an owl.

18

The stairs were extremely narrow. Matthew led the way down but had to turn almost sideways to avoid brushing against the sides of the passageway. Where the steps ended there was an arched opening with a tunnel disappearing into the gloom and it was immediately apparent that they would need to fetch a torch. Charles went running back to the house but when he returned a few minutes later Matthew was nowhere to be seen.

"Matthew?" he called. He began to descend the steps and shouted into the darkness, "Matthew?"

There was the sound of some coughing and spluttering, and Matthew emerged from the dark tunnel, brushing brick dust from his clothes.

"I was too excited to wait for you," he grinned, "so I thought I'd explore the tunnel on my own."

"Did you find anything?"

"No, it's too dark. Once you get inside, after a short distance the passageway turns a corner and there appears to be something blocking the way, but I couldn't tell what it was without the torch."

"Well, now we have the torch so let's take a look."

They began their descent and eased their way somewhat gingerly into the tunnel. As Matthew had said, the passageway soon turned a sharp right and then as Matthew shone the torch they realised that blocking their way was a closed wooden door. Matthew passed the torch back to Charles who, in the confined space, had to duck and weave to keep it trained on the door since Matthew was occupying the whole width of the narrow passage. Matthew turned the knob and pushed. It remained closed but it felt jammed rather than locked.

"I think that perhaps the door has absorbed moisture and expanded," said Matthew.

He pushed again, and then put his shoulder to it. At last, after several attempts with an increasing amount of brute force each time, the door finally admitted defeat and opened reluctantly with much creaking and the sound of wood scraping and splintering against the stone floor.

Moving slowly and cautiously, Matthew and Charles stepped inside. They were met with a blast of cold, salty air and became aware that the sound of the sea could once again be heard, somehow echoing from somewhere within the dark cavern.

Charles had been right; this was, indeed, a crypt.

Fortunately, as the beam of light from the torch swung left and right they discovered a dangling string which, when it was pulled, switched on a couple of rather dim light bulbs. As they looked about them, with everything bathed in this somewhat surreal glow, it became clear that this was quite a large underground chamber with a variety of passages leading from it. One, in particular, was the source of an icy draught and, to judge from the distant crashing sound which came from it, possibly led straight to the sea. Long years ago, numerous alcoves had been built into the walls and each now contained a coffin. Some of these were obviously very old indeed.

Despite the noise of the waves in the distance the place possessed a certain stillness, but the feeling of decay was unmistakable, and those areas which had once displayed some handsome blue paintwork were now, little by little, flaking and crumbling away as the ravages of time took their toll.

"*the blue cavern of an echoing deep,*" said Matthew, quietly. "Surely we must be very close to journey's end now."

As they had been moving around the crypt, Charles had noticed that some of the brickwork displayed elaborate carvings. In particular, each alcove had an animal engraved immediately above it. This one was a tiger; over there was a fish of some sort; and that one was an eagle, among numerous others.

"It would appear that we're supposed to become grave robbers," he said.

"You're surely not telling me we should be opening all these coffins," Matthew answered.

"Not all of them, no; just this one." He pointed to the alcove at the end of the crypt.

"Why that one, especially?"

Charles pointed to the animal which was carved into the apex of the arch above it, and said "*the slight lizard show his jewelled head.*"

Sure enough, the stone-carved creature was definitely a lizard, but both Charles and Matthew hesitated as they stood staring into the alcove and down at the coffin lid.

"Are we really going to do this?" Charles asked.

"If the sapphire really is inside that box we don't have any choice."

"But it might not be; like you said before, there might be just another roll of film waiting for us."

"That still doesn't give us any choice."

"True."

They knew they were going to break open the coffin. But still they hesitated.

"I can't believe that we're really contemplating this; it's like a scene from a Dracula movie."

"Do you think the lid will be nailed down?"

"Who knows? Only one way to find out."

A further hesitation.

"Let's not forget that there is a time limit to this whole ridiculous business," said Matthew, which was as much to increase his own fortitude as it was to encourage Charles to take action.

They each took a deep breath and, without another word, they took up positions at opposite sides of the alcove. Reaching inside, they carefully manoeuvred the heavy coffin towards the edge, inch by painstaking inch. Then, grasping one of the old brass handles fastened to each end, they gently lowered the casket to the floor. They then crouched and placed their fingers beneath the wooden rim which ran round the edge of the coffin. They looked at each other from their respective ends, hesitated for just one moment longer, summoned all their nerve, then nodded and suddenly stood up, bringing the coffin lid with them. Steeling themselves for a putrid stench and the sight of decaying flesh they lifted the lid and moved it sideways - and all but dropped it on the floor in surprise.

The coffin was completely empty.

Empty, that is, except for a small pouch made from thin black fabric laying serenely in the centre. Matthew immediately grabbed it and looked inside. Letting out a hopeful yelp he put his hand into the small bag and pulled out a small velvet-covered box. Charles stepped closer as Matthew slowly opened the lid.

And there, at long last, was the sapphire!

"Yes!" screamed Matthew. "Yes! YES!" His voice rang exultantly round the stone chamber.

Charles reached out his hand. "Let me see it."

He lifted it carefully from its container and held it up to the light. The gem was perfect. Even in this dim light its beautifully crafted facets both reflected and refracted the light in a way that was truly mesmerising. *We've done it,* he thought to himself. *We've actually gone and done it!* He heaved a sigh of relief and felt a rush of exhaustion suddenly descend upon him. There was nowhere to sit down, apart from either on the floor covered with stone dust, or on the edge of the alcove where the coffin had been. He opted for the latter.

Meanwhile, Matthew had reached into the black pouch again and this time pulled out a piece of folded paper. Written on Lord Alfred's personal stationery, bearing his coat of arms, and in the same cursive script which had provided them with that vital first clue several days ago, was a message:

> *"Congratulations, whoever you are. The fact that you are reading this message means that you have correctly solved the trail which I laid for you. Contact my lawyer, whose details are below, and all the necessary arrangements will be made. My final request is this: Please, please use the money wisely."*

Still sitting down, Charles gave a small laugh. "Well, it seems that we need to go and make a certain phone call." He reached forward to shake Matthew's hand.

"Not quite yet," said Matthew.

Charles looked surprised. "Why ever not? We've found the sapphire and solved the mystery."

"We need to have a little chat first."

Charles felt a cold shiver go through him. There was a steely edge in Matthew's voice which he hadn't heard before. He tried to retain a measured tone and said, "What's on your mind, Matthew?"

Matthew spoke in a slightly higher pitch now, and his eyes were a little glazed. "I've got debts, Charles; big ones. And the fact is, as I'm sure you would agree, that I am the rightful heir to my father's estate. How about if we went, say 80-20?"

In the same calm voice, Charles replied, "Matthew, we made an agreement. I do hope you're not going to try and change its terms now."

"But it should *all* be mine, shouldn't it? I'm his son. His son! I could go to 75-25 but that's my final offer. I need the money, Charles."

"Your father's fortune is so vast that even receiving half of it will set you up for life. If we hadn't made our agreement there is every chance that I might've found the sapphire ahead of you and then you would've received nothing."

"Oh yes, you're right. Poor little Matthew could never achieve anything on his own. Poor little Matthew always had to have someone to hold his little hand. Poor little Matthew always had to go running to Daddy for help!"

"Matthew, let's go back to the house and talk about this over a drink. We could both do with it." His voice stayed calm but he could feel the drops of sweat as they ran down the inside of his shirt. Matthew, his eyes fixed on Charles, took a step towards him, menacingly.

"You just had to get involved, didn't you? Why couldn't you leave well alone? Then everything would've been ok." He moved closer and his voice rose to a scream, "I'm the heir to Heston Grange! Me!" and then, with both hands reaching out for Charles' throat he hissed through gritted teeth, "and me alone!"

"I'm not so sure that's correct."

Matthew whirled round in surprise. The voice came from one of the dark recesses of the crypt.

"But you were correct when you said that we need to have a little chat."

"Who are you?" screamed Matthew. "Show yourself!"

A figure moved forward out of the shadows and stood in a pool of the dim light.

"Oh, dear. Whatever am I supposed to do with you? You don't even recognise your own father?"

Standing before an astonished Matthew and Charles, in good health and very much alive, was Lord Alfred Willoughby.

19

I t was as though time stood still. Neither Charles nor Matthew could quite believe what they were seeing. Lord Alfred said nothing but eyed them both with a shrewd gaze. Eventually, it was Charles, still perched on the edge of the alcove, who recovered his speech first. He spoke in a gabble, barely coherent.

"Lord Alfred...but I was there...I saw you. You -"

"Died?"

"Well...yes."

"To borrow that delightful quotation, 'the reports of my death were greatly exaggerated.'"

"What about the Will?" asked Matthew, his voice barely above a whisper.

"The Will? Ah yes, my Will. Wrong question, my boy. That's the wrong question. I had hoped that you might be pleased to see me; that there might be some glimmer of happiness at my still being present in this world. You might have asked me whether I was in good health and whether there was anything I needed. At the very least, you might have asked how it came to be that I had somehow managed to die and yet still be alive today. Even if you had simply feigned some interest, as a matter of common courtesy, at least that would have been something. But, no. Following my remarkable resurrection, what are your first words? 'What about the Will'." He sighed deeply. It was a sad, depressed sigh.

Charles found his voice again. "But how did you- ...*why* did you- ... you faked your own death?"

Lord Alfred smiled. "It was rather convincing, wasn't it? I must confess, though, by the day of your arrival I had practised it many times. I wanted to make sure I got it just right." He took a deep breath and then continued. "But I suppose I do owe you some sort of explanation. You're looking awkward, Matthew. Why don't you sit down?" he indicated the ledge where Charles was already seated.

"No thanks, I'll stand."

"As you wish." He thrust his hands into the deep pockets of his corduroy jacket and began to speak again, looking rather like a university lecturer, pacing slowly back and forth, moving in and out of the pools of dim light on the floor of the crypt as he did so.

"I am an old man. I may be a reasonably healthy old man, but I cannot escape the fact that I am still old. Having been blessed with the gift for making money, if indeed it has been a blessing rather than a curse, the final significant financial decision I needed to make was concerning the settling of my estate after my departure." He stopped his walking and focused his gaze on Matthew before continuing, "You don't need me to remind you that I had some concerns regarding this matter. Eventually, rather than simply give away a free handout, I hit upon the idea of turning it into a kind of challenge." He glanced again at Matthew, who was staring at the floor. "I was hoping against hope that the value of hard work and applying yourself to a task would somehow be realised. Was I really asking too much?"

He paused, and the distant sound of the sea echoed plaintively around the crypt.

"As you can imagine, it took quite some time to set up this little scheme of mine. I spent a long while searching through my poetry collection before I was able to find the perfect piece for use with this task. Once I discovered 'The Grave of Shelley' I was delighted. It was truly extraordinary how closely the lines of this poem matched the already existing features of the house and cemetery. The only ones I had to fabricate were the addition of the poppies in the panelling outside Meg's room, and the owl at the top of the steps leading down here; and I engaged a couple of local craftsmen some time ago to create them. But, as for the pyramid-shaped room under the eaves, the model sphinx and so on, it all fitted perfectly. The very finest author could not have scripted it better! Now, as you will have reasoned, I made both pieces of film several days before my - ahem - performance. Having thus ensured that all the relevant clues were correctly positioned along the way, I realised that once the wheels were set in motion I would need an 'inside man', an assistant who could help things along when required, as well as keeping me informed of any developments."

Matthew glared at Charles. "You were setting me up, all along!"

"No, yet again you are in error," said Lord Alfred.

"Then, who?"

"Come along, my boy, it doesn't take rocket science to work it out."

He looked incredulous. "James?"

Lord Alfred gave a sarcastic grunt. "Well done. I knew you'd get there eventually."

Then he turned to Charles.

"On the night of your arrival, you turned up before your appointed time! When James brought you to my room, I had only just managed to return from hiding the sapphire. While you waited outside, he helped me to change quickly, getting rid of my soaking wet coat, and told me that you'd seen my torchlight from your window. But I didn't bother to dry myself too thoroughly - I thought that the presence of a little extra moisture would add to the illusion of illness."

"But how did you get in here?" asked Charles. "You'd never have been able to move that flagstone all by yourself."

"Look around you. These underground chambers are extensive. You discovered that yourselves when you found your way into the pyramid room from beneath the lodge. They date back to when they were used by smugglers hundreds of years ago and there are, in fact, several entrances that I'm aware of. Who knows? Maybe there are still more waiting to be discovered - but I digress. Once I knew you had realised the significance of the Shelley portrait I simply made my way down here and waited for you to arrive. Oh, but please forgive me, I'm getting rather ahead of myself."

He cleared his throat and continued.

"Following my dramatic exit, the crucial thing was to make sure that you found your way to my tower room and the all-important first piece of film. I instructed James to hide the box containing the key in some place where he knew you would find it. I felt it necessary that you find it rather than he simply hand it to you, as a precaution to ensure that he was distanced from my scheme - in case you should ever suspect that he may have some deeper involvement in all this. Your first real test came after you viewed the film for the first time. I told James to suggest to you that you might consider embarking on the quest without advising Matthew at all - and I was there to hear your reaction."

"You were there? In the library?"

"Mr Seymour, the sprawling design of Heston Grange was not in any way accidental. Its irregular shape facilitated the inclusion of a good number of hidden passageways. Later on, I could show you some of them if you like." He smiled before continuing. "In fact, I did make a small blunder and you heard me as I moved around behind the oak panelling. Annoyingly, I was not as quiet as I had wished to be. Thankfully, on the spur of the moment James came up with some convoluted story about rats, and I managed to stifle a laugh. From my concealed position I heard the way you responded to his sugges-tion and knew that you were of good stock. It was pure good fortune that when you happened to hear me on a subsequent occasion, it coincided with the arrival of Mrs Gillcarey. I heaved a sigh of relief and decided to keep a safer distance from that moment on. So there was now nothing else for me to do but stay hidden and wait for you to solve the clues...and now here we are, having reached journey's end at last." He looked Charles in the eye and held his gaze for a long moment, and then glanced over at Matthew who fidgeted and looked at the floor.

"Just one final thing to say," said Lord Alfred, and his tone hardened. "This whole ruse was created and set in motion so that I could finally establish one thing, once and for all." He turned to Matthew again. "I needed to know for certain whether the reports I was hearing of your conduct were true or not. I needed to find out for myself whether you were truly worthy of the Willoughby name, not to mention the Willoughby fortune. I know, of course, that you had a troubled adolescence, and I admit that I was perhaps not always the best father in the world. But throughout this entire masquerade I hoped and prayed, day in and day out, that you would somehow show yourself to be a good man with a truly noble spirit. Instead, what do I find? No sooner is the mission accomplished than you turn traitor and immediately start to rescind on your agreement. And so, now that we stand at the end of the trail, I have reached my final decision. On my death - that is, my *actual* death - my estate will pass to you, Charles."

Matthew gasped. "This is a joke, right dad? Another of your little games?"

"With great wealth comes great responsibility, Matthew, and that is something which you have shown you do not possess."

Matthew looked like a man who had lost his strength and he staggered back against the wall. "But I'm your son!" Tears of anger welled up in his eyes.

"Even now, I hope that you might somehow learn the error of your ways."

"But I still get nothing, is that it? Nothing! While this - this imposter takes the entire fortune that should have been mine?"

"You could always try getting a job, if you know what that is, or perhaps you should get rid of that smart gleaming car that's parked out front - I don't suppose it's paid for yet, is it?"

Matthew threw back his head and howled with rage. It was the sound of years of built-up heartache and frustration bursting forth in a primal shriek, with its hideous tone reverberating and resonating, as it bounced off the stone surfaces and echoed throughout the crypt with an unnerving other-worldly quality.

Lord Alfred continued, "You could have had everything. Indeed, there were times when I wanted to you to have it all. But at least one of us needed to stay level headed enough to see the situation as it was, and deal with it appropriately."

"No!" screamed Matthew, the tears running freely down his face. "NO!"

He reached inside his jacket and Lord Alfred suddenly paled as he found himself staring into the muzzle of a Tokarev TT pistol.

"Against the wall, both of you! Now!" Matthew gestured with the handgun, and Lord Alfred and Charles slowly did as they were instructed.

"This is a stupid course of action," Lord Alfred blustered. "All you're doing is proving me right."

"Shut up!" There was a pause as Matthew, bristling with rage, regarded his two prisoners. Then he gave a small laugh.

"Remember what you said about the sphinx in one of your stupid films? - About how it would strangle people? Well, just to show you that I was actually listening and paying attention, you might like to know that's what gave me this idea. Of course, your unexpected appearance means I've now had to modify my plan a little, but it remains the same, in principal."

"You're speaking like a fool! Put the gun down and we'll talk."

"No! NO! For once, just once, you're going to listen to *me*. You got that?" He waved the gun again.

"Here's what will happen: in a few minutes time I shall be calling the local police. I'll tell them that as I was endeavouring to solve the next clue I happened to stumble across my father being killed by Charles Seymour who was trying to secure the entire inheritance for himself. I tried to duck back into the shadows but he saw me and I had no option but to shoot him dead in self defence."

"You're mad. Put the ruddy gun down while you still can!"

"Then, at last, that will be the end of these pathetic time-wasting games you've had us all playing, and I will be the sole heir to the Willoughby fortune, as is my right."

Charles glanced down at the open coffin which had until recently contained the sapphire. It seemed to yawn before him like a gaping chasm waiting to swallow him whole. He was trying to think; trying to decide what to do, but his mind was in such a whirl he could not order his thoughts in any coherent manner. Was this it, he wondered. Is this how my life is to end? In an underground cave with no-one to help?

"Oh, but you needn't worry," Matthew continued. "At each of your funerals I shall be the very epitome of grief. I shall weep and wail long and loud and no-one will be able to console me. Naturally, they won't realise that my tears will really be tears of relief – and triumph."

Lord Alfred smirked. "You won't do it," he said. "You're not man enough."

"Is that so? Well, Lord Alfred Willoughby, for once in your perfect little life perhaps your judgement is just about to display a flaw - a fatal one."

Then he stood firmly on both feet and levelled the pistol. Steadying his aim and breathing deeply, the next words came hoarsely from his throat, "Why didn't you love me?"

"Matthew?" Lord Alfred's voice was quieter now, calmer. "This is not the way. We can talk it through and work something out."

"Too late for that," Matthew replied, his face still wet with tears. "Too late for that, and now - it's too late for you!"

His expression was set and grim.

"Don't be a fool, man!" Lord Alfred whispered, pleading.

"Bye...Dad."

Charles closed his eyes.

Matthew surveyed the scene for just a moment longer...then squeezed the trigger. A sharp crack echoed throughout the crypt. Then he seemed to falter and stagger a little, before dropping his gun and falling to the floor spread-eagled and unconscious.

From the shadows behind him, James emerged and stood over him, still wielding the cricket bat. He glanced across at Charles, who was now as white as a sheet.

"I did warn you he was a scoundrel, sir."

20

Following a rather unpleasant and emotional trial, in which both Charles and Lord Alfred were the principal witnesses, Matthew Willoughby was sent to jail. James and Mrs Gillcarey sat in the public gallery of the courtroom as he was led away to begin his sentence. She dabbed a tear from her eye as she saw the overwhelming conflict of emotion crossing His Lordship's face.

It was not long afterwards that His Lordship fell ill and, finally, died - for real this time. The funeral was a simple affair, as he had requested, with only a very few people in attendance.

"He wanted to leave quietly and with as little fuss as possible," explained the vicar to the select gathering. Charles and James had exchanged glances at that moment, each knowing what the other was thinking - that Lord Alfred's first 'death' had been fraught with fuss and was anything but quiet!

As expected, when the Last Will and Testament was read, apart from the five million pounds which James received, along with Heston Lodge for Meg, Charles inherited everything else and suddenly found himself to be very wealthy indeed. He moved into Heston Grange and set himself the task of gradually refurbishing the more decaying areas, intending to restore the house to its former glory. He also invited both James and Mrs Gillcarey to retain their positions as butler and housekeeper and was delighted when they both agreed. However, his otherwise pure delight was slightly tarnished by a question that hovered in the back of his mind. So he decided to address it, and waited for an appropriate time, knowing that a suitable moment would present itself sooner or later. As things turned out, it was sooner.

It was a pleasant Summer afternoon, and Charles was relaxing in a cane rocking chair on one of his many patios following a delicious lunch of monkfish and fresh salad. The sun was shining, the birds were chirruping merrily, and even the ocean in the distance was sounding friendly today. James was just setting down a tray of coffee with steamed milk when Charles decided that now was the time.

"James, can I ask you something?"

"Of course, sir."

"Thanks to the provision of Lord Alfred, you are now a millionaire."

"Yes, sir."

"In the light of that, why would you wish to continue working as a butler?"

"Are you unhappy with my service, sir?"

Charles laughed, a full friendly laugh.

"Good gracious, no! It's just that most people, having encountered such a windfall, would probably stop working, or at least look to embark on something new."

"At my time of life, sir, is it not perhaps just a little on the late side to be looking for something new? In any case, I feel that I owe it to you to stay in your employment."

"Whatever do you mean? Why do you owe it to me?"

James shuffled his feet and looked a little uncertain. When he spoke, Charles knew that he was suddenly not speaking as a butler, but man to man.

"May I sit down, sir?"

"Of course. Let me pour you some coffee."

"No, thank you." He paused, and Charles knew that James had something significant to say.

"I need to tell you something of Lord Alfred's history," he began. "His Lordship was very close to his brother who was happily married and had four lovely children. Although Lord Alfred dearly loved Lady Caroline, his second wife, it seemed that they were unable to have children, for some reason. They were so deeply heartbroken after the death of their first adopted son, William, that His Lordship and his brother made a rather extraordinary pact: having had the privilege of raising a wonderful family of his own, but not wishing to have any further children it was decided, with the full agreement of all concerned, that this brother and his wife would have one more child which they would then give to Lord Alfred to raise as his own. The brother, though, had fallen on hard times and was not in employment. So His Lordship's part of the bargain was to offer him full time employment and to allow him frequent access to see the boy growing up; although, naturally, he was never allowed to mention his connection with the lad."

"What employment was he offered?" asked Charles.

James cleared his throat. "At that time," he replied, "there was a vacancy for a butler." he paused and looked down.

It took a moment for the penny to drop.

"James...you are Lord Alfred's brother?"

James nodded, slowly. "And Matthew is my son. At least, he was, for a short while. But can you even begin to imagine how difficult it was for me to see my son growing up in a way that was, shall we say, less than satisfactory? As time went on, with his conduct becoming steadily worse, both my wife and I began to feel so guilty that after having had such a wonderful family of our own we had now provided my brother with such a disappointing son. It seemed to hit Margaret - my wife - especially hard. And, although I can't be sure, I can't help feeling that Matthew's going off the rails was the initial cause of the start of her deterioration."

"She became unwell?"

"In a manner of speaking. What do you think? You did meet her, after all."

So here was the second thunderbolt.

"Meg?"

James nodded again, sadly. A tear slipped from the corner of one eye and began to run to down his cheek.

"As her condition worsened I felt so powerless to help. So she was moved to the lodge. I wanted to do whatever I could; I would have done anything, but there was nothing that could be done. In a way, I felt as though I was abandoning her, but - oh, Mr Seymour - it was because I loved her so much that I could not bear to watch as she gradually ceased to be the lovely, caring person she had been before. I still visit her occasionally, when I think I may be strong enough to keep from breaking down in front of her. But then..." the tears were flowing more freely now as he fought to maintain his composure, "... but then it occurs to me that if I am the sort of man who would abandon his wife like that..." his voice cracked a little. "...then maybe it's not so surprising that Matthew, my son, would turn out to be such a bad sort."

Charles reached out and placed his hand on the old man's shoulder and offered him a tissue. He waited quietly and respectfully as James wiped away his tears.

"Thank you for telling me all this, James. I very much appreciate it."

An appreciable silence ensued, broken only by some occasional birdsong or the buzzing of a passing winged insect.

Eventually, James spoke again.

"Shortly before Alfred passed away," he said, "he gave me something to pass to you - at a time of my choosing which I considered to be a 'suitable moment'. I think that perhaps that time is now."

He reached inside his jacket and produced an envelope, which he handed to Charles.

"What is it?"

"I have only a vague idea. May I be excused for a while, sir? I will be back presently."

"Yes, of course. Please take as much time as you need."

"Thank you, sir."

James disappeared back into the house and Charles was left alone. He looked down at the envelope in his hand and took a deep breath.

There had been enough shocks for one day and he didn't especially want another. What would he find inside?

A little nervously, he opened the envelope and removed the folded paper. There were several sheets, all bearing Lord Alfred's distinctive coat of arms and his unique handwriting, and at a glance he could see that this was quite a long letter. But, as he unfolded and straightened it the opening words hit him like a kick from a mule:

My dear son, Charles,

In an instant, he felt as though all his strength left him and the letter fell back onto his lap. It can't be, he thought. Surely it can't be. After some considerable time, with a rapid heartbeat and trembling fingers he lifted the letter and began to read again.

My dear son, Charles,

Firstly let me assure you that, no matter how fanciful this may seem, you are indeed my son - although I realise that this news will come as a shock to you. Your mother was my first wife. We underwent a rather hostile divorce when you were still a babe in arms and I was denied all access to you; and I know that throughout the time when you were growing up she would not even speak to you about me. I felt my heart would break, but I resolved to follow your development as closely as I could.

Charles' eyes were so full of tears that he could hardly focus, but he persevered.

So, when you took part in your school plays I was there, sitting at the back. I also used to watch your sports days from the vantage point up on the hill - you remember the one? You used to so much enjoy climbing it. Later, although your mother was reluctant at first, she eventually allowed me to pay your fees for you to study law. I was so proud of you when you excelled at your studies and passed your exams with such high marks. And, when you graduated, I managed to watch from a distance as you had your photograph taken in your smart scholarly robes, but I had to always make a point of slipping away early from such occasions before anyone recognised me.

Before I married Caroline, my second wife, she confided in me that she was not able to have children. Then and there we decided that we would adopt. Our first son, William, was the apple of our eye. When he had his motorcycle accident it almost tore us apart but we persevered and set all our hopes in our second boy, Matthew. By now, you will know that his biological parents were James and Margaret. Well, remembering our little experience down in the crypt, you now know at first-hand what manner of man he became. But try to imagine, if you can, how this affected not only myself and Caroline, but also James and Margaret as well. It was a trial which seemed to become more and more difficult to endure with every passing day. And, once he left home, I never saw him - unless he needed money.

Once you became a practising solicitor I was so pleased that you elected to stay in the vicinity and I took every opportunity I could to engage your services. True, you were expensive (you thought I didn't realise that?) but I was so pleased to see how efficiently and methodically you undertook your work. As my Last Will and Testament underwent its numerous revisions I began to have serious doubts about wanting to leave anything at all to Matthew; I knew he would squander whatever I gave him. But you were a different proposition altogether. And yet...don't ask me how, I still cared deeply about Matthew and just could not find it within myself to cut him out of my will altogether. I can still see him as that charming little boy from all those years ago. Eventually though, I hit upon the idea of the 'cryptic lines' which, as it turned out, provided what I consider to be a very satisfactory outcome, having given all concerned a fair crack of the whip.

I was there that day, and I heard when you expressed surprise and asked James why I had included you in my Will. Well, my dear Charles, now you know: it was not a contest between son and solicitor, but between two sons. So I salute you, the eventual winner. I'm not going to ask you to use the money wisely, because from the depths of my heart I know there is no need. It is in safe hands.

Just one other thing, if I may. I was sorry to learn that you had been left high and dry by your fiancé, but please don't despair; wounds such as these will be healed by the passage of time and, somehow, I don't think it will be too long before you find love again.

And, finally, for all those years when I could not be there for you, I ask your forgiveness. I deeply regret all those things we did not have the opportunity to talk about, all the places I was not able to take you and all the time that we might otherwise have spent together. Yet, as much as I was able, I was there, looking out for you and feeling so very proud to know, even privately, that you were my son. And what greater thing can a man ask than that?

With all my love, always,
Dad.

Charles reached for another tissue as, not far away, James and Meg sat together on the sofa in the tiny sitting room at Heston Lodge, not speaking but quietly holding hands. On the coffee table in front of them, with only a few cracks visible, sat the recently repaired sphinx. Meg, with half-remembered recollections floating hazily through her mind, had a gentle smile on her wrinkled face as she gazed wistfully into the depths of a large blue sapphire.

--The End--—

ABOUT THE AUTHOR

Richard had long cherished the idea of writing fiction ever since, while still a child, he attended an English Literature event with the author, Leon Garfield. However, life took another path and his training was in a different field: he studied at the Royal Academy of Music for five years, between 1984 and 1989, graduating with high honours and a recital diploma – the only guitarist in eight years to be awarded such an honour – and winning the Julian Bream prize. As Richard neared the end of his studies in London, he helped to found the TETRA Guitar Quartet – an ensemble with which he remained for over thirteen years, giving concerts all over the world and releasing four CDs to great critical acclaim.

In his own right, he has appeared on television and radio numerous times and his many solo performances include playing before Princess Anne at St James' Palace. He has also played for the English National Opera orchestra, in addition to acting as coach and musical consultant on a number of plays and musicals in London's West End.

He composed the incidental music to Chekhov's *Three Sisters*, recently seen in London's West End, directed by Michael Blakemore and starring Kristin Scott Thomas, and subsequently broadcast on BBC4 television, and his music for *Rumplestiltskin* received over 300 performances in its first year alone. Another of his musical productions, *Kennedy*, was three times nominated for the RUTAC Drama

Awards. He has also recently completed a five-volume set of pieces for solo classical guitar.

In addition, to being in constant demand as a teacher and adjudicator of musical festivals, Richard has also branched out internationally, writing for the Chinese Orchestra of Hong Kong. To date, two commissions have been premiered there: "*The Fiery Phoenix*" and a concerto for xylophone entitled "*The Rise of the Dragon Prince*". In 2008, Richard was elected Associate of the Royal Academy of Music (ARAM), and he travels globally as an examiner for the Associated Board of the Royal Schools of Music.

His musical adaptation of "*The Brothers Lionheart*" premiered at London's Pleasance Theatre, followed by a successful run at the Edinburgh Festival. Future projects include an adaptation of "*The Selfish Giant*", by Oscar Wilde, besides a number of other chamber compositions. Richard's first novel, "*The Cryptic Lines*" has now been adapted for the stage; and his song "*Until You're Safely Home,*" having been premiered by the Military Wives Choir in the UK has since been performed all over the world, as well as featuring as part of the Canadian Military Tattoo in Ontario.

A native of the Lake District, Richard now lives in a leafy suburb of south London, where he has recently completed his next novel, "Order of Merit," but he still relishes the occasional opportunity to ascend some of the more remote Cumbrian mountains!

For further information, or to contact Richard directly, please visit his website:

www.richardstorry.com

Printed in Great Britain
by Amazon